THE JUMPER

A Rick Rose Novel

Mike Paull

WHAT THEY ARE SAYING ABOUT THE JUMPER

This is the third book in Mike Paull's "Rick Rose" series, and it did not disappoint. I was on the edge of my seat as I read each page and couldn't put the book down until I reached the very end.

Mike's skillfully crafted main character, Rick Rose, is a lovable, endearing guy that the reader can't help but root for even when he's being his own worst enemy. This author's books are always well researched and professionally written. His detailed descriptions of various settings and his obvious knowledge of the legal and forensic matters necessary to write such stories are exceptional. I am looking forward to the next installment in this entertaining, suspenseful, mystery series.

—Ann Marie Jameson, author, *Willow Rose Series*
Hammond, LA

It's been four years and two novels since Rick Rose, a certified dentist and recovering alcoholic, reluctantly accepted the job as forensic odontologist with the San Francisco Medical Examiner.

The Jumper, like previous Rick Rose novels, has many laugh-out-loud moments inside a fast-paced mystery that will keep you guessing until the very end. So, buckle up and enjoy another fun read from Mike Paull. The author does not disappoint.

—Lynn Solte, author, *Lydia's Story*
Hollywood, FL

Mike Paull has written another cracking yarn featuring Dr. Rick Rose, forensic odontologist, working for the San Francisco medical examiner. Rick, as we have seen in previous books, has an obsession for not letting the dead remain nameless and thus often crosses the boundary between his work and police detective work. In *The Jumper*, Mike Paull has produced another page turner which will not disappoint fans of whodunnits. He knows how to twist the plot so that surprises continue until the very end.

—Jack N. Lawson, author, *Criminal Justice*
Basse Normandie, France

THE JUMPER

A Rick Rose Novel

Mike Paull

"A half truth is a whole lie."

—*Yiddish Proverb*

DEDICATION

For Kyrie on your 21st birthday - **12/22/45**

PROLOGUE

Bruno Cappelletti knew how hard it was to pick up a decent fare at three in the morning; most people hailing cabs at that hour are either drunks or deadbeats. It was too late to hang out in front of a hotel or restaurant, so as much as he hated burning the gas, he decided to cruise the Embarcadero—a boulevard connecting San Francisco's eastern piers.

He was old enough to remember when this was a neighborhood where people thought twice about going out late at night, but urban renewal had taken care of that. Now high-rise condos lined the boulevard and overlooked Fisherman's Wharf and Pier 39.

Bruno slowed as he passed Wharf Landing, an expensive condominium complex that sold out six months ago in the spring of 2023. His eye caught a uniformed attendant opening one of the double glass doors. Instinct signaled him to stop. He braked and backed into the building's white zone.

A man who looked to be in his early forties, wearing jeans and a down parka, hobbled out. In one hand he held a soft leather briefcase and with the other he waved in Bruno's direction. Bruno flipped on the interior lights and popped the lock on the passenger door. The man looked back at the building, then slid into the rear seat.

"Ya okay, sir?" Bruno asked. "Ya look really pale."

"I'm fine … just too much champagne at the party. Let's get out of here. Okay?"

"Sure, where to?"

"Just drive."

Bruno took off and hung a left back onto the boulevard. "I gotta start the meter."

"Fine. Would you have a towel by any chance?"

"Yeah, to clean up after the drunks."

"Could you hand it to me?"

Bruno passed it back. "You're not gonna puke in my cab, are ya?"

"No, I … I spilled a drink all over my shirt at a party." He stuffed the towel under his parka, then fiddled with a cigarette and despite a shaky hand managed to get it lit. "Is that the Golden Gate Bridge up ahead?"

"Yeah, ya going to Marin?"

"Yes, to … to Sausalito."

"No problem. I'll dispense with the travelogue then?"

"Please." The guy took a long drag and let the smoke out through his nose. "So … so why're you working this late, anyway?"

"Family. One kid in college and another getting ready."

"Every night?"

"Workin'?"

"Yeah, you do this every night?"

"Every night but Monday. Nobody goes anywhere on Monday."

The man nodded and slipped his hand under his coat. He winced, leaned back and closed his eyes.

During the ten minutes it took to reach the bridge, the temperature dropped a good five degrees, low enough to reach the dewpoint. A thick layer of fog had formed. Bruno squinted, as if that would help him see through the cloud and make it easier for him to spot the approach lane. He drove onto the bridge and seeing no other traffic, put his foot on the gas.

The man felt the acceleration and opened his eyes. "Go ... go slower."

"Limit's forty-five."

"I ... don't care, just slow up."

Bruno figured the man was unaccustomed to riding in thick fog and dropped down to thirty as he approached the bridge's mid-span.

"Pull over," the man said.

"What? I can't do that."

From the back seat, a pistol came through the opening in the glass. "I said, pull over ...please."

Bruno looked in his rear-view mirror. Outside all he saw was fog, but inside he was able to catch sight of his passenger. The man's face had turned from pale to ashen gray and he was sweating profusely. Bruno coasted to a stop.

The man in the back seat wedged his briefcase through the opening. "For your kids' college," he said. Then the rear door flew open and while holding one hand against his chest, he limped to the railing and put one leg over the top. He turned back at Bruno with an anguished look. "Be careful," he yelled and disappeared into the fog.

CHAPTER ONE

A ny idea what you call a dentist who gets caught drinking on the job? How about unemployed? That was me in 2019. Six months later, I graduated summa cum laude from an AA program, but my patients weren't the least bit impressed. They'd already found other dentists.

Every day I take a minute to stare at the plaque on my office door: *Rick Rose D.D.S. Forensic Odontologist.* It looks good and it sounds a lot better than unemployed. You see, for the last four years I've spent a lot of time in the morgue, working for Dr. Alexandra Keller, the chief medical examiner for the city and county of San Francisco.

This morning was a typical summer day in the city. It was cold and it was foggy. As I do every morning, I joined the line in front of Josie's Java truck and waited to pick up a couple of lattes—one for me and one for my secretary, Stella.

FYI, Josie is my ex. She bought the truck from Big Louie, the previous owner. I only mention this because I gave her the money to buy it without any stipulation she'd have to pay it back, and yet she's never offered me so much as a dime of discount on the coffees.

"Next," said a familiar voice. I took two steps forward.

"Oh, hi, Rick, you're late today."

"Yeah, you have any whipped cream left?"

"Saved some just for you. The usual?"

"With a little hazelnut."

When the steaming cups arrived, I pulled out a twenty. "I'm curious, why don't I get a discount?"

"You want one?"

"No, just wondering why you never offered."

"I'm saving up to pay you back. If I start giving discounts, I'll never build a nest egg big enough to do it."

I couldn't argue with her logic and handed her the money. "Keep the change ... for the nest egg." I walked away with the lattes and the strange feeling that I was somehow paying myself back.

When I stepped into my office, Stella was eagerly awaiting her daily caffeine fix. She relieved me of one of the lattes and took a sip. "Oh, Rick, that's so good," she said. "Whipped cream and hazelnut."

"I think Josie gave us an extra spritz of both."

We sat down and worked through the topping to get to the coffee. "What happened with you and Josie, anyway?" Stella asked. "She seems really nice."

"Yeah, she is, but let's not go there. Okay?"

"Oh, sure, sorry. None of my business. I didn't mean to ..."

I held up my hands. "Don't worry about it, I'm good. So, what's on the schedule for today?"

"Dr. Reingold called at nine sharp and asked if you'd come down to the morgue ASAP. I figured that meant after our coffee."

"You figured right. Everything's a crisis with Helmut."

"And Dr. Keller wants you to stop by."

Whenever I have a choice between Alex Keller, my boss, or Helmut Reingold, our pathologist, I always choose Alex. Besides marveling at her intellect, I enjoy being in the company of a woman with shimmering red hair and beautiful green eyes. Her secretary told me to go right in. I knocked once and stepped inside. "Good time?" I asked.

She looked up from her computer. "Perfect. Have a seat. Coffee?"

"No thanks, full up. Stella said you wanted to see me?"

"Yes, a new John Doe checked in late last night."

"No ID or fingerprints?"

"Nothing. No wallet, no papers, and prints didn't match any of the databases."

"I'm guessing that's why Helmut is tracking me down."

"Probably and expect the homicide captain to call you too."

"Mike Kelly? Why? Was the guy murdered?"

"If you weren't in recovery, I'd pour you a stiff drink."

"That bad, huh?"

"The guy jumped off the Golden Gate Bridge."

Something didn't add up; at least thirty people make that leap every year and that's why a barrier is under construction. "Since when is committing suicide considered murder?" I asked.

"The guy didn't die from the fall."

"Drowned?"

Alex shook her head.

"Okay already, are you going to tell me or not?"

"Looks like he died from a gunshot wound to the chest."

CHAPTER TWO

M y satellite office is located three floors below my executive office. It's in the basement. It's the morgue. The very first time I stepped out of the elevator and got a whiff of the Clorox and formaldehyde, I lost my lunch. It hasn't changed much since. I still hate that smell but manage to hang onto my last meal.

Today the elevator doors opened, and a new stench was in the air—like somebody spilled a bottle of aftershave. I quickly made my way to the morgue, punched in the security code and stepped inside. The smell was the same, but the ambiance was different. Helmut, a classical music freak, had Debussy's "Clair De Lune" playing through the overhead speakers. Ironically, none of his guests were listening.

Helmut looked up from the operation he was performing on a recent check-in and gave me a wave to join him at his desk. "Hey, Rick, thanks for coming right down."

I didn't think it necessary to mention I'd already had two stops before him. "Yeah, no problem. Say, what's with the woodsy odor down here?"

"You like it? I added some pine scent to the ventilation system."

I wrinkled my nose. "Kinda smells like someone died in the forest."

He laughed and pointed at a row of stainless-steel drawers. "I want you to meet someone."

I followed him to drawer 26A, where he slid it out and lifted the sheet off a corpse. It was hideous. The skin was purple, the facial bones were broken, and the limbs were twisted in awkward positions. On the right side of the chest, just below the breastbone, was an elliptical hole about five millimeters wide.

I swallowed hard. The latte I'd had earlier was on the move and its direction was straight up. "That the jumper?" I asked.

"You heard?"

"From Alex. The purple skin ... bruised from the impact?"

"No, you can't bruise when you're dead and he was before he hit the water. That color is from the pooling of blood after death. Called livor mortis."

"How do you know he was dead when he hit?"

"The livor mortis. Hitting the water from that height is like hitting concrete. There would have been horrendous bruising if he was alive. The only true bruising he has is around the gunshot wound."

"Alex said he's a John Doe."

"That's what the police say. You think you can find something we can link to dental records?"

"You know the drill. We can chart the dentition, but we can't cross-check it with every dental office in the country. We'll need more than that for a positive ID."

"But you're going to check out his mouth, right?"

"That's what Alex pays me for. When are you doing the autopsy?"

"Tomorrow morning. He's all yours after that."

~ * ~

Mike Kelly, the full-time captain of homicide and part-time boyfriend of Alex, greeted me, as always, with a firm handshake. "Thanks for stopping by. How about a latte? My secretary picked up a couple."

I was still working to hold down my last one. "No, thanks, but you go ahead."

Mike, always the perfect gentleman, declined also. "I'm sure you've heard, we have a real doozy on our hands this time," he said.

"Yeah, I just came from the morgue. How is it this guy died from a gunshot wound in the middle of a suicide plunge?"

"Good timing, I guess. He didn't have to look down."

"Neither one seems like a good option. So, no ID?"

"None. I'm hoping your exam may find something to go on."

"Don't count on it."

"I won't, but I can hope."

"So, how did our guy get to the mid-span anyway?" I asked.

"There are only two possibilities, either he used the walkway or was dropped off by a car. I doubt, with the severity of the gunshot wound, he could have walked. That leaves a car."

"Maybe he was murdered before he got there and someone threw him off the bridge."

"That's what we thought but a woman who was driving by in the middle lane, saw him climbing the railing."

"So, she must have seen the car that brought him."

"That's the problem. The fog was like waves of pea soup and the woman was concentrating on staying in her lane. A movement at the railing caught her eye for a split second. She recalls seeing a taxi, but with the thick fog she couldn't say for sure if it was parked or just moving slowly in the right lane."

"Obviously, you haven't had a call from a cabbie."

"Obviously."

"How about the cameras?"

"Fog blurred most of the footage, but we have partials on three cabs that crossed in that time period."

"License numbers?"

"No, just blurred images, so you can see why I'm hoping you find something for us to go on. When is your exam?"

"Tomorrow morning. I'll let you know if I come up with anything."

Mike stood, signaling the end of our conversation. "You know, I'm going to have to put a detective on this case," he said.

"Yeah, I know."

"You think Alex would be okay with Jim Allen?"

A few years back Alex dated Jim Allen and it ended badly. Now, he is her least favorite homicide detective. Until last year I wasn't fond of him either. He struck me as a self-centered, arrogant prick who went out of his way to avoid hard work. Circumstances changed and so did Jim Allen. Last year he came across the country to bail me out of a tight spot I'd gotten myself into in Arkansas and we became friends, not best buddies, but friends.

"She should be good with it," I said. "But I'll run it by her anyway."

"Thanks, just so she's not blindsided."

CHAPTER THREE

I hopped off the Powell-Hyde cable car at Union Street and walked the half block to my house on Russian Hill. I glanced up at the front window and caught sight of a familiar face. It was Einstein, my cat.

Anyone who has ever lived with a cat knows they are totally bipolar. For those who haven't, let me enlighten. I never know which Einstein will greet me—the loving, licking, purring Einstein or the angry, aloof, where's my dinner Einstein.

Today turned out to be the latter. As soon as I opened the door, he vaulted off the windowsill and strutted toward the kitchen. When he sensed I wasn't following, he stopped and turned his head, as if to say, "Well, are you coming?"

I shrugged and followed him to the refrigerator, where I took the lid off a can of liver and chicken *pâté*. Finally, I received my first meow. While Einstein slurped up the feline delicacy, I called my next-door neighbor, Jacques Devereaux.

Jacques graduated from the Sorbonne medical school in Paris around the same time as I graduated from the UCLA dental school in Los Angeles. While I went directly into private practice, Jacques came to the U.S. and did a psychiatry residency at Stanford. I met him when I moved to Russian Hill. He answered on the first ring. *"Bonjour, mon ami."*

"Damn it, Jacques, you're in America. It's just, 'hi Rick.'"

"I know, just pulling your bracelet."

"Chain ... pulling my chain."

"Okay, okay, chain. What's up?"

"You want to grab some pasta at Frascati?"

"I don't know, I wanted to finish a book I'm reading and ..."

"I'll buy."

"Oh, in that case, when?"

"Half an hour. I'll bang on your door."

"We walking?"

"It's only a block away."

"Just pulling your bracelet. See you in half an hour."

I was incorrect when I said Frascati is only a block away. It's actually only a half a block and it took us all of three minutes to get there. The maître d', wearing a black tux with an open white shirt, met us at the door. *"Buonasera, Dottore Rose, Dottore Devereaux."*

"Hey, Matteo, we come here every week, isn't it about time you call us Rick and Jacques," I said.

He looked around to see if anyone was within earshot. "Thanks, Dr. Rose, but not in front of the *capo*."

"Capo?"

"You know, the boss, eh?"

"Oh, yeah, no problem."

Matteo led us to a table in the corner that he saved for his special customers. "Just for you ..." he glanced around, "... Rick and Jacques." The front door opened, and he scurried off to greet the next customers.

Jacques ordered a glass of cabernet, and I asked for a Ritual Old Fashioned, a zero-proof whiskey that they stocked just for me. "I'm getting the octopus salad and the pappardelle," I said. "You?"

Like most psychiatrists I've known, Jacques took an unusual amount of time to make a simple decision. Finally, he said, "I think the tomato bisque and the *steak au poivre*." I began to laugh. "What?" he asked.

"Only you would order an all-French dinner at an Italian restaurant."

He shrugged. "So, why are you springing for dinner?"

"I just thought it would be a nice neighborly gesture."

"So, you're not looking for a psychiatric opinion or anything like that?"

"Of course not," I took a slug of my artificial whiskey. "But since you mentioned it ..."

"Hold it. Does this free dinner include dessert?"

"It can, if you like."

"Okay, let's have the question."

"The new John Doe I'm working with has me stumped. He was shot in the chest and instead of going to the hospital, he jumped off the Golden Gate Bridge. Any idea why a guy would do that?"

Jacques gave me the stereotypical, "hmm."

"Hmm? What's with the hmm?"

"That's what we do to justify three-hundred and fifty dollars an hour."

"Well, then, give me about ten minutes worth of hmm's."

"Hmm ... I have no idea."

"Come on, you're a psychiatrist, give me something."

"Okay, the guy was committing suicide."

"Why? The bullet was already going to kill him."

"Did he know that?"

"I don't know what he knew."

"Well, the guy obviously had issues."

"What kind of issues?"

"How would I know? I never met the guy."

"I'm reneging on paying for this dinner and that includes dessert."

"You can't, you invited me."

"Then give me something."

"Okay ... hmm ... a wise man once said, 'It's a capital mistake to theorize before one has data. Insensibly one begins to twist facts to suit theories, instead of theories to suit facts.'"

"That's impressive. Was that wise man from your list of medical school professors?"

"No, he was from a Sherlock Holmes novel. Say, if you don't mind, I'm going to change the subject. Are you in a serious relationship with anyone?"

"You mean romantically?"

"Yes, romantically."

I never asked Jacques if he had a preference for men or for women. I figured it was none of my business, but now ... "no, I hope you're not thinking of propositioning me?"

He smiled. "Don't worry, you're not my type. Boobs are too small."

"So, why the interest in my love life?"

"I have a colleague, a woman I went to medical school with, who just moved to the states. She doesn't know anyone here and I was thinking maybe you ..."

I wrinkled my nose like a kid who had just been served a helping of Brussels sprouts. "I dunno, Jacques, I've never had good luck with fix ups."

"She's smart, nice looking and comes with a French accent."

"I'll think about it."

After dinner was over, the waiter set a silver plate on the table with an upside-down check on top of it. Jacques grabbed it. "Tell you what," he said. "Instead of you treating me tonight, save it for a dinner with Francoise. If you don't enjoy her company, I'll pay for that dinner too."

"You get the check and I'll give it some thought."

CHAPTER FOUR

T he next day, I made sure to drop by Alex's office before visiting the morgue. She was buried in her computer with only a few strands of flaming red hair showing above the screen. "Hey, Boss," I said. "You're going to fall in if you get any closer."

She looked up, pulled her readers off the tip of her nose and gave me a warm smile. "Hi, Rick, what brings you up here first thing in the morning?"

"Oh, nothing much."

"Uh-oh."

I laughed. "Well, there is one thing."

"Should I sit or stand?"

"You're fine. Mike Kelly wants Jim Allen to work with me on our new John Doe case."

"What did you tell him?"

"That it was your call."

"Do you need him?"

"I need someone with a badge."

"Can you keep him out of my hair?"

"I can try, can't promise."

"Well, that's good enough for me."

"You sure? I can ask Mike for someone else if ..."

"I'm good, really."

I doubt she really was good with it, but Alex is a lot smarter than I am. When she decides, I don't question. Instead, I asked, "What's on your schedule this afternoon?"

"Why, what do you have going on?"

"John Doe's initial exam."

"You need my help?"

"I could do it by myself, but I like bossing an older woman around."

She rolled her eyes. "I'm forty-five. How old are you?"

"Uh ... technically I'm thirty-nine, but I'll be forty next week."

"Well, if you stop calling me an old woman, I'll take you to dinner for your birthday."

Wow, I'd just scored a twofor. Not only did I get Alex to assist with the exam, but I got a dinner date with her too. "Deal," I said. "Meet you in the morgue at noon."

~ * ~

I've been doing this job for almost four years and you'd think by now I'd feel comfortable in the morgue. I don't. I was never really trained to be a forensic dentist; I just lucked into it. So, for me, it's always been on the job training or more accurately put, trial by fire.

I stumbled and bumbled my way through my first cases, struggled with the smell of formaldehyde, and more than once prayed to the porcelain god. All too often I hid behind a false bravado that got me in over my head and I've lost count of the number of times I've been beaten up by bad guys. I threatened to quit several times, yet here I am, still in the morgue working on patients who have two things in common: they're dead, and there's no name to put on their gravestones.

Helmut was sitting at his desk eating a sandwich and reading an article titled, *Autopsy in the 21st Century.*

I took the chair across from him. "What's changed?" I asked.

He lifted his head out of the paper. "Oh, hi, Rick, what d'ya mean, 'what's changed?'"

"The autopsy. What's changed from the twentieth century?"

He pointed to the article. "Oh, that. Nothing, really."

"So, why read it?"

"Well, I guess ... huh, it's just what pathologists read."

I decided this conversation was going nowhere and changed the subject. "Speaking of autopsies, did you finish John Doe's?"

"About an hour ago."

"And?"

"Like I thought, he died of a gunshot wound to the chest."

"What kind of gunshot?"

"Don't know yet. The bullet was lodged in the lower lobe of his right lung. I sent it to the ballistics lab."

"Anything else of interest?"

"Oh, I almost forgot." He opened his top drawer, took out a plastic baggie and handed it to me. "This was on his little finger."

I moved the ring around in the bag without having to touch it. "What is this thing anyway? It's huge."

"Yeah, looks like he won the Super Bowl or something."

"Can I take it with me?"

"You know the rules. Take as much time as you like with it, but evidence has to stay here."

"Okay, I'll check it out later. When can I go ahead with my exam?"

"Whenever you like. I sewed him up and left him on

the surgical table for you."

I thanked Helmut and changed into scrubs, a surgical mask and gloves. Then set up my laptop, the charts, examination instruments and portable x-ray unit. Before I could peel back the sheet covering John Doe, Alex stepped into the room. "Give me a minute to change," she said, as she slipped behind the privacy screen.

Even though Alex was used to seeing fall victims, she cringed when she looked down at this one. The livor mortis that Helmut described earlier covered John Doe's entire face with a bluish-purple color.

"You okay?" I asked.

"Yeah, sure. Just gets to me every time."

Alex wasn't new to these types of exams, she'd assisted me with many. I adjusted the bright overhead lamp and we got right down to work. I used a small mirror to scan the mouth and an explorer to poke around the teeth. Then I called out each tooth number and its description for Alex to chart.

We were done with the tooth exam in ten minutes. Alex turned on my computer, attached the x-ray cables, and handed me the sensors and the handheld digital unit. Together, we snapped eighteen images of the teeth.

"That was quick," Alex said.

"We're not quite done."

Alex looked as if she wanted to scratch her head, but the latex gloves got in the way. "What's left?"

"Soft tissue."

"I thought you already looked at that."

"Not in depth. Hand me that surgical headlamp, would you."

I strapped it around my forehead and hooked the battery pack to the side of my belt. When I turned it on, the

60,000 Lux illumination looked like a laser beam moving in the same direction as my head. I used the mouth mirror to spread each cheek and focused the light on the tissue. It looked normal—as normal as dead tissue can look. I moved my head to direct the light at the soft and hard palate, nothing remarkable there either.

"Almost done," I said. I handed Alex a metal retractor. "Deflect the tongue a little; I want to feel under there."

She used the tool to reach under the right side and pull it away from the teeth. I poked two of my latex covered fingers under the tongue to the floor of the mouth. It felt smooth, like the outside of a rubber inner tube. "Normal," I said. "Let's check the other side."

Alex retracted the left side of the tongue and I stuck my fingers under it. "Uh, oh."

"What?"

"There's a lump under there. Pull on that retractor so I can aim the light in." Alex pulled hard against the tongue to give me visual access. "Wow, it's raised and at least four centimeters long."

"That's over an inch and half. What do think it is?"

"Well, it could just be a swollen sublingual salivary gland, but they don't usually get this big. I think it's a tumor of some sort."

"Cancer?"

I shrugged. "Maybe, maybe not. We'll have to excise it and get it under a pathologist's microscope. I'm going to need Helmut's help."

"I'll get him," Alex said.

While I waited, I closed my eyes and thought about my histology class at UCLA dental school. Now I wish I'd paid more attention, but in those days it was like a melatonin fix that put me to sleep as soon as the professor began to speak. I remember feeling like I'd died and gone to heaven when Dr. Dzieduszycki took pity on me with a 'C' minus.

Helmut jolted me back to the present. "I brought a scalpel and a specimen jar," he said. "You want to remove it, or should I?"

I held out my hand like I was making an introduction. "He's all yours."

He was quick. Two incisions, a curette to pry the growth from the underlying tissue, and into the specimen jar. "I'll have a report for you tomorrow," he said.

CHAPTER FIVE

After Alex's relationship with Jim Allen ended, or should I say exploded, he became *persona non grata* around our office. But as I mentioned earlier, life has a funny way of turning things around. Now, I kinda like the guy; Alex, however, still can't stand him. Since my office is on the second floor and Alex's is on the third, I figured so long as Jim only pushes the number two on the elevator panel, I can keep him out of Alex's hair. We'll see.

The intercom buzzed. "Detective Allen just arrived," Stella said.

I told her to send him in and Jim lumbered into my office with a cigarette hanging from his lips. "Any ash trays around here?" he asked.

"I doubt it, this building is non-smoking."

"Since when?"

"Well, I've been here almost four years and it's always been."

He put the butt out on the bottom of his shoe and wrapped it in his handkerchief. "Huh, sorry about that. So, how can I help you ID this guy?"

"Mike Kelly said a witness thought the jumper got out of a cab, but with the thick fog on the bridge that night, she couldn't be sure. Let's go over the camera footage and see if we can find anything."

"I thought that'd already been done."

By now I knew Jim really well. Vinegar never motiv-ated him, but sugar always did. "Some desk jockey looked at them," I said. "But you're a field detective. If there's something to be found on those tapes, I'm pretty sure you'll find it."

He smiled. "Yeah, sure, I'll look at the footage with ya. When do ya want to do it?"

I looked at my watch. "I have a doctor's appointment this afternoon. How about I meet you at the station to-morrow after lunch?"

"Sounds good."

After Jim left, I stepped into the reception room. "What's up, boss?" Stella said.

"How about I buy you a drink after work?"

She looked at me over the top of her glasses. "Are you dating again?"

"Not, yet. I'll meet you in front of MoMo's at five."

~ * ~

I have a love hate relationship with MoMo's bar and grill. I love the ambiance, but I hate the memories. It's lo-cated right across the street from Oracle Park and is usu-ally jammed with Giants fans. It's also the place where I received the only 'Dear John' letter of my life.

Tonight, the team was in L.A. playing against the Dodgers, so the only fans hanging around were those waiting for the seven o'clock telecast. We took seats at the end of the bar.

"How can you sit at a bar without ordering alcohol?" Stella asked.

"It's easy, booze almost ruined my life. I won't let it do it again. But, hey, you order anything you like. I'm okay with it."

"You sure?"

"Positive."

"Well, maybe a Cosmo, but light on the vodka."

The bartender slipped a couple of cardboard coasters in front of us. "Hey, Doc, haven't seen you in a while. Who's this beautiful young lady you brought with you?"

If you were looking for a poster boy for the surfing industry, this would be your guy. He looked like Brad Pitt with a tan and a ponytail. He even had a first name synonymous with the monstrous waves off half Moon Bay. "Maverick, this is my colleague, Stella," I said.

He stretched out his hand. "Hey, Stella, my pleasure."

Stella's cheeks got a little rosy and she held onto his hand a little longer than she normally would. "Nice to meet you, Maverick. But I'm not really Rick's colleague, just his secretary."

"Well, if the doc says you're a colleague, I'm going with that. What can I get you?"

"Uh, a Cosmo, heavy on the vodka."

He turned to me. "O'Doul's? Non alky?"

"Great."

Maverick stepped away to fill the drink orders and Stella picked up a bar napkin to dab a couple beads of perspiration from her forehead. "Wow, that guy's very good looking."

"Really? I never noticed."

"Is he hooked up, do you think?"

"I don't know. Want me to ask him?"

"Oh, God no, he'll think I'm interested."

"Aren't you?"

"Sure, but I don't want him to know it."

"Why not?"

"Rick, you don't understand women. Some men don't like aggressive ones."

Stella was right, I don't understand them. The only two serious relationships I've had in my life ended badly —one with divorce and the other with a Dear John letter. "That's what I want to talk to you about," I said.

"You have a new girlfriend?"

"No, a buddy wants to set me up on a blind date. I'm curious, is that sort of thing still in vogue?"

"Well, nowadays, most people use dating apps instead of fixups."

"Isn't that just a blind date using a ten-year-old photo of yourself?"

Her face took on a pensive expression and she looked up at the ceiling. "I never thought of it that way. I guess it is ... kinda. So, who does your buddy want to fix you up with?"

"A French woman."

"Oh, they're sexy."

"How do you know that?"

"Ever see a Dior perfume ad?"

"Those are models. This woman's a doctor."

"Well, I'll bet she's good looking. What's her picture like?"

"I told you, this is a blind date, I have no idea what she looks like."

"Oh, okay, so what kind of doctor?"

"Not sure. My buddy's a psychiatrist, so ..."

"Oh, be careful, I went out with a psych major once and all he talked about was 'my mother this' and 'my mother that.'"

"Okay, other than don't talk about my mother, should I know anything else?"

"No sleepover on the first date."

"Got it. Don't talk about my mother and no sleepover. Anything else?"

"Don't order scampi."

"What? Why not?"

"Too much garlic. Your breath will smell awful when you kiss her goodnight."

Before I could re-summarize the instructions, our drinks arrived and so did Stella's red cheeks.

CHAPTER SIX

The police station housing the homicide division was about a ten-minute walk or a five-minute jog from the medical examiner's building. I chose the ten-minute option.

Homicide occupied the entire fourth floor and was arranged in a chain of command. After checking in with the front desk officer, I passed a half dozen secretarial desks before reaching ten detective cubicles. Beyond them was the inner sanctum—Mike Kelly's private office.

I spotted Jim in the second cubicle. He was talking on the phone while puffing on a cigarette. "Yeah, babe, ten o'clock's good … and wear something I can see through." He hung up and saw me standing next to him. "Oh, hey, Rick." He winked. "Just lining up an interview."

"Sounded like it," I said, and took the seat next to him. "So, did you get ahold of the CCTV footage?"

"Sure did." He moved his computer monitor to where we both had a vantage point and tapped a few keys on the board. The screen lit up with: *GG Bridge cam #1, 08/22/23*. "What's the timeframe we're looking for?"

"The witness guessed at about three-thirty a.m. Let's look thirty minutes before and thirty after."

Jim tapped in 0300 and hit PLAY. Images appeared in

shades of black and gray, but with all the fog blowing by the camera they were mainly gray.

"Which camera is this?" I asked

"The toll plaza on the south end."

"Good. Our guy went over the east railing, so he would have been going north from this spot. Right?"

"Unless he was going the other way and decided to dart through six lanes of traffic to jump off his favorite side of the bridge."

I used to live in Marin County and know tolls are only collected on the Golden Gate Bridge from southbound traffic. That means northbound cars don't have to stop on entry and are going at a healthy clip when they pass this point. "I can't make out the cars in all that fog. Can you slow it up?"

Jim tapped the slo-mo key. "We're looking for a taxi. That right?"

"Right."

The slow motion helped a lot. We were able to get a good five second look at each vehicle. At 0321, I said, "Hold it, I think I saw something."

Jim hit the BACK arrow and then STOP. The silhouette of a sedan showing through the fog filled the screen. I pointed a pencil at it. "Is that a roof light?"

Jim squinted. "I think so. Looks like a Toyota but I can't read the plate."

"How about the logo?"

"Fog's too thick."

On a post-it, I jotted down *0321 Toyota*. "Okay, let's keep going."

Jim tapped PLAY and the footage began moving again. He slowed it down. About thirty vehicles, mostly trucks, came into view during the next fifteen minutes.

None of the four door sedans appeared to have roof lights. At 0336 a roof light appeared through the fog. Jim hit STOP and backed it up. "Is that an 'F' on the door logo?" he said.

I peered into the screen, hoping my gaze might be able to pierce the fog. "And a 'C'," I said. I wrote down *0336 F-C*. "Keep going." Another ten minutes later we both yelled at the same time. Jim froze the frame at 0347 with the image of an American four-door displaying a blurred decal on the driver's door. "Crown, that's the name of another cab company," he said.

I added it to my list. The next thirteen minutes yielded only twelve vehicles and none were cabs.

Jim closed the CCTV folder. "What d'ya think?" he said.

"Can you get Google on that old Dell of yours?"

"Hell, yes. It's not that old."

"Bring up a list of cab companies operating in the city."

He tapped, tapped again, and then hit PRINT. His equally old Epson spit out a piece of paper. He looked at it and handed it to me: *ABC Taxicab, Crown Cab, Eco-Taxi, Fog City Cab, Green Cab, National Cab, Yellow Cab.*

I ran my finger down the list. "Crown Cab for sure and …F-C, for …Fog City."

"Yeah, but that leaves five others that may be driving Toyotas."

I looked at my watch, it was a little after four. "It's getting late. How about first thing tomorrow, you take Crown and Fog City. I'll call the others to see who was using Toyotas that night and maybe by the end of the day we'll have some drivers to interview."

~ * ~

When I got home that evening, my roommate was at the window nervously waiting for me to appear. I gave him a hug and he returned the affection with a tongue swipe that felt like a Brillo pad across my cheek.

After dishing out a can of Fancy Feast Gourmet Salmon to my buddy, I took out the blender and poured in some coconut milk, a squeeze of lime, some orange juice, a few chunks of pineapple, and a bunch of crushed ice. Twenty seconds later I felt like I was in Hawaii.

One thing about drinks without alcohol, they go down too fast. I set the glass in the sink and before taking a shower, speed dialed Jacques on my phone.

"*Allô, mon ami,*" he answered. I didn't respond. "Rick, is that you?" he asked.

"Is Jack there?"

"Come on, Rick, I know it's you."

"Oh, I thought I was calling Paris for a moment."

"Okay, okay ... no French. What can I do for you?"

"I decided to take you up on your offer. Give me her name and her number."

CHAPTER SEVEN

Most mornings I have a five-to-ten-minute wait for lattes at Josie's Java truck, but today there was no line at all. I approached the window and peeked inside. She was in the corner with her head in her hands. "Hey, Josie, what gives?"

She looked up, dried her eyes and shuffled over to the window. "Oh, hello, Rick."

"What's wrong?"

"Nothing."

"Something is."

"I ... I can't talk about it."

"What?"

"I can't."

"Come on, let it out."

"I ... I lost some money."

"Lost it? Like you dropped it on the way to the bank?"

"I invested it."

"Invested? In what?"

"Crypto currency."

My heart sank. Josie's a smart person, but finance and investments were never her long suit. She'd earned money at a part time job when we were married, but after our divorce she lived off an inheritance from her grandmother until it ran out. Her economics resume and her bank account were both pretty thin. That's why I loaned her the money to buy the coffee truck. "Who, may I ask, talked you into that?" I asked.

"One of my customers. He's a broker."

"Stockbroker?"

"Maybe. I don't know, just a broker, I guess."

"How much?"

"Did I lose?"

"Yeah, how much?"

"Nine thousand, nine hundred—almost all I had saved to start paying you back."

I could see this conversation was pushing her to the breaking point and I knew giving her a lecture would only shove her over the edge. "Don't worry about it," I said.

"But now it'll take forever to pay you back."

"I don't need the money, Josie. Take this as an expensive course in money management and move on. You'll be fine."

"But ..."

"Do you have enough to keep the business running?"

"I, I think so."

"How much do you have in the bank?"

"About four thousand dollars."

"You'll be fine."

"You sure?"

"Look, you have two choices. You can let this thing destroy you or you can let it motivate you. How about you sell some coffee to that line that's forming behind me?"

She peeked around my shoulder and wiped her eyes. "Thanks, Rick, why did I divorce you, anyway?"

"We can talk about that another time." I put a twenty on the counter. "Two large lattes, extra whipped cream."

As I started to leave, I turned back. "Josie, do you have that broker's business card?"

"I think so, why?"

"Not sure, just give me his card."

~ * ~

Stella was at her computer, but I knew she wasn't working. She was trying to look busy while waiting for her caffeine fix. When she unpacked the paper bag her eyes lit up. "Yes, you got the big boy cups today."

"Gotta support the local merchants."

We both skimmed off the whipped cream and licked the spoons clean. "So, did you call that French gal?" Stella asked.

"Not yet. Alex said something about dinner this week."

"So what? You can't go out twice in one week? Besides, Alex is a boss dinner not a date dinner." I didn't respond and Stella cocked her head like the gears were falling into place. "Well, isn't it?" She must have read the stupid look on my face. "Rick, don't tell me you're still carrying a thing for Alex."

"Of course not." I stood and headed for my private office. "Hey, I have a big day. Buzz me if Jim Allen calls."

I sat in front of my computer and pondered Stella's question. Would I love to have a close emotional relationship with Alex? Sure. Did I think that would ever happen? No chance in hell. I grabbed my phone and opened 'new contacts'—Dr. Francoise Barbier, 415-555-0127. Then I hesitated; maybe later, I thought.

I had five taxi companies on my list: *ABC Cab, Econ Taxi, White Cab, National Taxi, Yellow Cab.* I googled their phone numbers and started with the first one.

A woman who cracked her gum twice as she answered, said, "ABC ... name and pickup address, please?"

"My name is Dr. Rick Rose from the medical exam ..."

"Address?"

"I'm not calling for a cab, ma'am."

"Well, you've reached a cab company, sir."

"I know. Do you use Toyotas?"

"Do I use what, sir?"

"No, does your company drive Toyota four doors as taxis?"

"Who's this again?"

I could see this wasn't going to work. "Rick Rose from the police department," I said. "Does ABC drive Toyotas? Yes or no, ma'am."

"Uh, no."

"Thank you. Goodbye."

I ruled out Econ Taxi. They said they drove Toyotas, but only Prius models. The image we had seen on the CCTV was definitely not a Prius.

White Cab gave me my first lead. A man with a husky voice, who sounded more like a driver than a receptionist, said, "Yeah, we got thirteen Toyotas in the garage—nine of them Camrys and four of them Corollas, but a couple are broke down."

"Were any in service on August 22nd ... at three in the morning?"

"Listen, Dr. Rhodes, you sound legit, but I can't give you that info."

"Rose, not Rhodes."

"Pardon."

"It's Dr. Rose. And why can't you give that out?"

"I dunno. Privacy act or some shit like that."

"What if a police detective came by your place? Would you give it to him?"

"If he has a badge?" He thought about it for a few seconds. "Yeah."

National Taxi turned out to be a limo service that only drove Cadillacs, Lincolns and Mercedes'. That left Yellow Cab, who had no reservations about giving out information. They had several Toyotas in their fleet, but none were operating after two a.m. on August 22nd.

I gave Jim a call. "Is this the Mouth Mechanic?" he answered.

"I thought only Alex called me that."

"I wouldn't know, we don't talk much."

"So I've heard. What did you come up with?"

"Crown said we can talk to their driver before his shift tonight. He works graveyard."

"So, about eleven?"

"Ten forty-five, but only for fifteen minutes."

"What about Fog City?"

"Their guy will be there for the swing shift tomorrow afternoon. How about you? Any luck?"

"White Cab drives Toyotas but won't give out any information without seeing a badge. Maybe we can swing by tomorrow after Fog City."

"Sounds good. So, tonight, ya want me to pick you up?"

"What time?"

"Ten fifteen."

"Sure, see you then."

CHAPTER EIGHT

I usually hit the sack around eleven, but not to-night. After tucking Einstein into bed—mine that is—at nine-thirty, I decided to suck it up and make the phone call.

She answered on the second ring, with a charming accent "*Allô?*"

I was out of practice for making dates over the phone and I'm sure my voice gave it away, but I hung in there. "Oh, uh, hi, Francoise, my name's Rick Rose ... uh, Jacques Devereaux gave me your number and ..."

"Yes, yes, Rick. Jacques said you might call."

"I hope it's not too late."

"Not at all, back in France we'd be just getting ready for dinner."

I smiled and hoped it would transfer to my voice. "Yeah, I was in Europe once and could never get used to that. Speaking of dinner, would you be interested in going out for one this week?"

"That would be wonderful, Rick. I hate to admit it, but my calendar has been wide open since I've come to the states."

"Great, how about tomorrow?"

"Tomorrow would be fine."

"You have my number on your phone. Text me your address and I'll pick you up at seven. Unless that's too early?"

She laughed. "Seven is perfect. I'm looking forward to meeting you. See you then and thank you, Rick ... for the call."

I hung up, breathed a sigh of relief and checked the time. It was getting late; Jim said ten-fifteen. I grabbed a jacket and went outside to wait for him.

Cops must get a great deal on black four-door sedans with cheap rims. Even though the detectives' cars are unmarked, it's a dead giveaway when they pull up; other than the police department and maybe PG&E, nobody would buy one. Jim leaned over, popped the passenger door and I slipped in. I wrinkled my nose. "What?" Jim said.

"Smells like an Indian casino in here."

"What's that supposed to mean?"

"Like cigarettes, stale cigarettes."

"Don't be such a pussy. So, who takes the lead?"

"You mean with this cabbie?"

"Yeah, ya want me to start?"

"I think so. If he's reluctant to talk, the badge might intimidate him into loosening up."

"That's what I figured too."

Crown Cab is located in the Bayview-Hunters Point district, an area I wouldn't step foot in at night unless I was with a cop. Fortunately, I was. Jim pulled up in front of a fenced lot that looked more like a prison than a car storage. Coiled razor wire ran along the top of the fencing and a push button call box was cemented next to the gate.

Jim pushed the red button and a voice came through the scratchy microphone. "Private property, Mac. I suggest you move on."

"And I suggest you open the gate, asshole. I'm with the police department."

"You have credentials?"

Jim noticed a camera on a post above the call box. He opened his wallet and held his badge toward it. "Open the fuckin' gate or you'll be spending the night with a bunch of drunks in the vomit tank."

A loud buzz came through the speaker and the gate opened. Jim laid a strip of rubber, drove into the lot and screeched to a halt in front of a sign that read: Office. "Now I'm in a bad mood," he said.

"Take it easy. Remember our mission. It's not to beat the shit out of a dispatcher."

Jim lit a cigarette and let a cloud of smoke out through his nose. "Yeah, you're right."

The room was filled with a bunch of drivers—some apparently ending their shifts and others beginning. An older man with a three-day stubble and a toothpick between his teeth greeted us. "Hey, man, sorry about that, lots of bad guys push that button at night."

The temperature in Jim's boiler had cooled. "No problem." He flashed his badge again. "We're here to talk to one of your drivers." He took out a matchbook with a name written on it. "Name's O'Leary. First name Sean."

The man pointed to a table where five men were playing pinochle. "The guy with the cap," he said.

By now we were the center of attention and the dealer slipped the cards back into a cardboard case. Three of the men drifted off to talk to the dispatcher. The guy with the cap and another man stayed seated. We sauntered over.

"You Sean O'Leary?" Jim asked.

The cabbie sat up and stiffened his back. "Who's asking?"

Jim flipped open his wallet and showed his badge yet again. "Detective Allen ... SFPD." He nodded in my direction. "Dr. Rose from the medical examiner's office. Mind if we sit down and ask ya a few questions?"

Sean's buddy made a quick exit and Sean shrugged. "Whatever," he said.

We each pulled out a chair and Jim cut right to the chase. "We understand you were driving last Thursday's graveyard."

"Yeah, so?"

"So, do you remember a fare that you took over the Golden Gate around three-thirty?"

The driver thought for a moment. "Hey, man, I have a lotta fares and I drive over that bridge every night. What's to remember?"

It was obvious this guy didn't like Jim, so I joined the conversation. "Listen, Sean, you're not in any trouble here. We just have to know if you made a stop in the middle of the bridge."

He smirked. "A stop? In the middle of the Golden Gate Bridge? Do I look nuts?"

"Not really, you look pretty smart to me."

"Smart enough to know it's illegal to stop on the bridge. Thousand buck fine."

"What if a guy slipped you a couple hundred, would you take the chance?" Jim asked.

"No way. Hey, who said I stopped on the bridge anyway?"

"No one," I said. "Your cab was caught passing the CCTV at the south end. That's all."

"Well, I didn't stop on the bridge. Okay?"

"You're sure you didn't stop?" Jim asked again.

Sean stood up and gave Jim the finger. "Fuck you," he said and walked away.

When we were back in the car I turned to Jim. "What do you think?"

"He's telling the truth. Pretty sure of it."

"Yeah, I thought so too. Maybe one of the guys from the other two cab companies will have something for us tomorrow."

The cable cars stopped running at eleven, so Jim parked in the middle of the street to drop me off. "See ya tomorrow," he said.

Before I got out, I took a business card from my pocket and handed it to him. "Ever run into this guy?"

He looked at the card: *Hans Van den Brink, currency broker.* "Never, why?"

"Just curious."

"You want me to check him out?"

"Would you?"

He jotted the name and address on the back of a matchbook and handed the card back to me. "Sure, no problem."

CHAPTER NINE

Jim dropped me off a little after midnight, but by the time I'd unwound and managed to fall asleep it was closer to two a.m. I slept right through my alarm and didn't get to the office until ten the next morning. Stella was looking at her watch as I walked in. "I told you not to stay overnight with that French lady," she said.

"I haven't even met her yet, we're going to dinner tonight."

"Oh, I was hoping for some racy details, but I guess it can wait."

"Well, you're going to have to wait a long time. Ever hear the rule, 'never kiss and tell'?"

"Sure, but I've never met anyone who followed it. So I guess I don't get any dirt or any coffee this morning."

"Sorry about the coffee. I'm late for an appointment with Helmut."

"That's okay. Anything special for me to do today?"

"Just your usual, but stay off the dating apps."

When I stepped into the morgue, Helmut was at his desk working through a report. "Is that for me?" I asked.

He looked up, startled that he wasn't alone. "Oh, Rick, didn't hear you come in." He handed the four-page document to me. "As a matter of fact, it is. Looks like you uncovered something interesting."

I sat down next to him and began reading through the pathology summary of the lump taken out of the jumper's mouth. Like all these reports, it was written to impress the reader. Latin terms were used even though plain English would have worked just fine—*cranium* instead of head, *glossa* instead of tongue, and *glandulae* in place of glands ...

I skimmed through the technical jargon, without admitting to Helmut that I didn't understand a lot of it, until I came to a familiar anatomical name written in English—sublingual salivary gland.

I backed up and read the entire paragraph. *Adenoid Cystic Carcinoma (ACC) of the sublingual salivary gland is a rare malignant tumor, characterized by slow growth, perineural invasion, local recurrence, and potential for distant metastasis.*

I set the report on the desk. "So, our John Doe had cancer," I said.

"Yup, a bad one. This one's so rare that by the time they find it, it's usually spread to the lungs or the liver."

"Do you think he knew he had it?"

"Hard to say. Normally, a surgeon would excise the entire salivary gland and then do radiation on the surrounding tissues, but obviously his gland was still in place so ..."

"So, maybe he didn't know it was there?"

"Or, maybe he knew and didn't want any treatment."

"Why would he not want treatment?"

Helmut threw up his hands. "You'd have to ask him that question."

I closed my eyes and tried to picture the face of this poor guy when the doctor told him. "Let's assume he knew he had the tumor," I said. "Which specialist, most likely, would have made the diagnosis?"

"Either an otolaryngologist or an oral maxillofacial surgeon."

"I know what an oral surgeon is, but what's an otolaryngologist?"

Helmut laughed. "That's a fancy name for an ENT doc."

Even though I didn't understand much of the report, I knew what I didn't know. One thing I did know, however, was how to use Google. "Can I take this copy?"

"Sure, I can print out another."

~ * ~

The swing shift is the tweener one. Beginning at 3 p.m. and ending at midnight, it's a part time day job and a part time night one. Jim and I showed up at the Fog City Cab company at two-forty-five. It was a much friendlier environment than the one we were in the night before. The neighborhood was better, the inside lighting was softer and the driver we wanted to interview was a college-educated guy who was driving to pay for a master's degree he was working on at the University of San Francisco.

"We'll keep this short," Jim said. "We understand you were working graveyard last Thursday?"

"Yes, sir, I usually work swing, but I took a double shift that night."

"Do you remember taking a fare over the Golden Gate Bridge?"

"The dispatcher told me to check my log and yes ... I had two trips over the bridge that night."

"Do ya remember them? Man ... woman?"

"I don't, wish I did, sorry."

"I understand, but the only one we're interested in is the one around three-thirty. Anything out of the ordinary happen that you might recall?"

"I'm sorry, I'd like to help you but ..." He shrugged.

I decided to let out the elephant in the room. "Did you stop on the bridge that night?"

The young man's brows lifted about a quarter of an inch. "Stop? No, sir. You can't stop unless there's an emergency."

"Did you have an emergency?"

"No, sir, I'd certainly remember if I did."

We thanked him and returned to the front of the building where Jim had left our car parked in a red zone. A meter maid must have come by, there was a ticket under the driver's wiper blade. Jim tore it up and tossed it into the gutter.

We headed for our last stop, the White Cab company, the one that wanted to see a badge before giving out any information.

Jim turned toward me. "That last guy was totally believable."

"For sure," I said. "How far to White Cab?"

"Next block."

The man at the desk was the same guy I'd talked to on the phone. "Yeah, I remember you, Doctor Ross, wasn't it?"

"Close enough," I said. "This is Detective Allen."

On cue, Jim opened his wallet and flashed his gold star. "We'd like to talk to any of your drivers who had fares across the Golden Gate between three and four a.m. last Thursday, the 22nd."

The guy looked at the badge and when he was convinced it was authentic, took out a twelve-inch-square, four-inch-thick binder and flipped through it two pages at a time. When he reached the date and time we were interested in, he ran his finger down the page. "Only one of our guys fit."

"That's fine," Jim said. "Can we talk to him?"

"Well, actually … you can't. He called in sick on the 23rd. Been out for almost a week."

"We'll need his home address."

The man jotted it on a piece of paper and handed it to Jim. "Thanks," Jim said. "But we'll need his name too.

"Oh, sorry, it's Bruno, Bruno Cappelletti."

CHAPTER TEN

I left the office early to get ready for my date with Francoise. I'd never spent time in the company of a French woman and I felt a few butterflies flitting around inside my stomach. It was the same feeling I used to have in dental school, when midterms snuck up on me and I knew I wasn't prepared.

I calmed my nerves by telling myself this wasn't an exam and the only preparation needed was the selection of a good restaurant. It certainly wouldn't be French; Francoise sounded like a woman who wouldn't want to go out and eat in her mother's kitchen. Italian didn't seem right either; being from Europe, she'd probably had her fill of Italian food. Then a novel idea hit me; how about a restaurant that served American cuisine?

When Josie and I were first married, we came from Marin County into the city almost every weekend and one of our favorite spots for dinner was the Hayes Street Grill. It always featured an eclectic fish menu, but it also had local favorites. I doubted Josie would mind so I made a seven-thirty reservation for Francoise and me.

Francoise had texted me her address: 1155 Jones. It wasn't lost on me that it was on Nob Hill, the most exclusive district in downtown San Francisco. I counted down the minutes on my Uber app and when it said 'arrived,' a new blue Mercedes pulled to the curb. I must admit I selected Uber Lux rather than my usual, Uber X.

Francoise spared me the task of taking an elevator to the sixth floor and roaming the hall for her apartment number; she was waiting outside and impossible to mistake. Dressed in slacks, jacket, kitten heels and very little makeup, she had an effortless elegance, a trait many European women seem to possess. I was thinking about using the only French word in my vocabulary—*bonsoir*—but instead, I said, "Hi, I'm Rick."

She gave me a peck on each cheek. "*Allô* Rick, call me Frankie."

"Frankie, that's so, so perfect. I love it."

She put her arm inside mine and we walked to the car. "I'm famished," she said.

I hope maître d's make a good living, they certainly deserve one. It had been five years since I last had dinner at the Hayes Street Grill, but when we walked in, James gave me a smile and said, "Dr. Rose, we've missed you." He didn't comment on the absence of my ex, instead he said, "May I take the lady's wrap?" He seated us in the back of the dining room, where I remembered the quiet tables were located.

The waiter arrived and asked if we'd like drinks, Frankie deferred to me. "Beaujolais, Bordeaux or Napa Valley?" I asked her.

"Napa, of course."

I turned back to the waiter. "Rombauer Chardonnay for the lady and a Luminara Chardonnay for me." He jotted the order on a pad and started for the bar when I stopped him. "Oh, and do you still serve the smoked trout toast with radishes?" He nodded and I held up two fingers.

"You don't prefer the Rombauer?" Frankie asked.

"I have a problem. Luminara is from Napa, but without alcohol. It's pretty good."

The drinks arrived and we tapped glasses. "Welcome to America," I said and we dug into the appetizer.

"*Mon Dieu*, this is wonderful," she said.

When the waiter returned and asked for our dinner selections, Frankie looked at me. "I trust your choices, Rick."

I wanted her to experience a California dish, so I chose two orders of the Fort Bragg, Petrale Sole with California-grown mushrooms.

"I have never heard of this fish—Petrale," she said.

"I didn't think so. It's found mainly in the Pacific Ocean and never in the Mediterranean."

"And this Fort Bragg? It's where the army is?"

I smiled. "Back in the 1850s, maybe. Now, it's a beautiful little town on the Mendocino coast, about two hundred miles north of here."

"I love that name," she said. "It has a beautiful rhythm. Men ... do ... cino."

"Tell you what, if you can stand my company tonight, we'll drive up there some weekend."

"Rick, that sounds wonderful."

I waved my finger as if scolding. "Like I said, 'if you can stand my company.'"

"And as you say in America, 'so far so good.'"

I told her about my past: my marriage, my fall into the rabbit hole filled with alcohol and my rebirth as a forensic odontologist. She shared with me her failed teenage marriage, medical school at the Sorbonne and the psychiatric postdoctoral fellowship she's doing at Stanford. We didn't leave the restaurant until after eleven. When I walked her to the front door of her apartment house, we hit that inevitable first date dilemma—to kiss or not to kiss? I decided less is more and offered her my hand.

She pulled her hand away, put it behind my head, and drew my face close to hers. "Have you ever had a French kiss?" she asked.

"I … I think so."

"Not like this." And she proceeded to lay one on me. When our lips parted, she said, "Do you want to come up?"

Stella's words of wisdom echoed through my brain 'don't talk about your mother, don't eat garlic and don't sleep over on the first date.' "I'd like to," I said. "But my romance consultant advised against it."

She laughed. "And who is this romance consultant?"

"My twenty-six-year-old secretary."

"Well, tell her she is a very wise woman. Goodnight, Rick. I enjoyed tonight, very much."

CHAPTER ELEVEN

An Uber ride to work takes only twelve minutes but costs me almost twenty bucks. The Powell-Hyde cable car only costs eight bucks and takes the same twelve minutes to get downtown. However, I then have a fifteen-minute walk to my office in the South of Market neighborhood—an area locals call SoMa for short.

After my date the previous night, I was feeling energetic. I grabbed the pole on the outside of the cable car, hopped onto its outside platform and rode downtown while taking in the salty sea air. By the time I reached Josie's Java truck I felt like I'd had a good day's workout. I didn't think it a good idea to tell Josie I'd been back to one of our old haunts, so I kept last night's dinner to myself. "The usual," I said." She whipped up the lattes in about two minutes and handed them to me in a paper bag. "Man, you're getting good at this" I said.

"Thanks, Rick ... and thanks for propping me up yesterday. Self-pity sucks."

"You don't need to thank me, we all need a kick in the ass once in a while."

"Well, thanks anyway. Say, I'm having a few people over to the house on Saturday evening. Any chance you could stop by?"

I didn't know how to answer. Was Josie asking me to be her date or just asking me to stop by as payback for helping her? I didn't want to hurt her feelings, but I also didn't want to send the wrong message. I liked Josie, but I had no desire to rekindle the old relationship. "Oh, darn, I have to go to San Diego for a conference."

She waved it off. "No problem, maybe another time."

"Yeah, another time, maybe."

Stella giggled when I opened the office door. "What?" I asked.

"Your hair's standing up like you put your finger in a light socket."

I licked two fingers and patted it down. "I rode on the outside of the cable car. Kinda windy out there. Here's your latte."

"Oh, goody." She peeled off the cover and licked the cream from the top. "So, how was the date?"

I fanned the steam coming off my drink. "Date? What date?"

"You know what date, with the French woman."

"Oh, that date. Fine."

"Fine? That's it? Fine?"

"It was good."

"Good or great?"

"Great, actually."

"Tell me about it."

"No."

"Why not?"

"Would you tell me about all your dates?"

She wrinkled her nose. "No, but ..."

"But what?"

"But if you tell me about your date, I'll tell you about my date with Maverick, the bartender."

"How did he get your number?"

"My guardian angel gave it to him. Thanks."

"You're not mad at me?"

"Of course not, I was hoping you would."

Let's face it, I don't understand young women. Stella was adamant about not giving Maverick her number for fear of appearing too aggressive, but she set me up to do just that. I looked at my watch. "Gotta go. We can finish our girl talk later."

My cell buzzed; I checked the caller ID. "Jim, are you here?"

"Yeah, I'm out front. Trying to stay clear of your boss."

"Okay. Be right out."

I jumped into the passenger seat of the black sedan and pinched my nose with my thumb and forefinger. Jim gave me a dirty look and flicked what was left of his Marlboro out the window. He put the car in gear and took off. "I checked out that Van den Brink broker guy for ya," he said.

"And?"

"He's a small time grifter. His real name is Homer Hanson, but he changed it a couple years back after doing a two-year stint in Lompoc. Why the interest in him?"

"It's personal. Thanks for the info. So, where does our cab driver live?"

"In the Sunset district, out near Ocean Beach."

"Does he know we're coming?"

"Yeah, I called him. Told him it was about a traffic violation."

Bruno Cappelletti answered the door in a pair of faded Levis and a sleeveless undershirt. He looked at Jim, who was holding up his badge, and then at me. "What?

Two guys to do traffic duty? Guess one to hold the ticket book and one to hold the pen." He laughed and held out a palm, signaling us to come inside. Jim and I took seats on the couch and Bruno flopped into a well-used La-Z-Boy. "So, what did I do, pick up a fare in a red zone?"

"We understand you've been out sick for a week," Jim said. "Anything serious?"

"Nah, just a little of that arthritis in my back."

"Well, that's good. Let me introduce ourselves. I'm Detective Allen from homicide," he nodded toward me, "and this is Dr. Rose from the medical examiner's office."

The smile on Bruno's face disappeared and for the first time I noticed a slight twitch in his left eye. "Homicide? Medical examiner? What the fuck?"

"We understand you worked the graveyard shift last Thursday, the 22nd," Jim said.

"Yeah, so ..."

"You took a fare over the Golden Gate Bridge."

"Did I? Don't remember."

"Your cab was captured on the CCTV at the south end."

"I don't think that was me."

"Do you work for White Cab?"

"Yeah."

"Well, your dispatcher looked it up. You took a guy across the bridge around three-twenty."

Bruno wiped his sleeve across his upper lip. "Oh, yeah, I remember now. Took him to Sausalito."

"You sure?

"Yeah, yeah, nice guy, big tip."

"Why did you stop in the middle of the bridge?"

"Stop? I didn't stop."

Now it was my turn. "Mr. Cappelletti, I examined the

body of the man who was in your cab that night. He jumped off the bridge. You stopped to let him out."

"No, no, I took him to Sausalito."

"Did you know your passenger had been shot in the chest?"

"Shot? No way."

"Your log said you picked him up on the Embarcadero. Is that right?" Jim asked.

"I guess. I dunno, I can't remember."

"That's what you wrote in the log."

"Okay, I picked him up on the Embarcadero, then."

"After you stopped on the bridge, did you see him jump?" I asked.

"No."

"No, you didn't see him jump?"

"No, I didn't stop."

Jim stared at Bruno for about thirty seconds, but it seemed more like five minutes. "A witness saw you stop and saw your passenger get out and go over the railing."

"What are you guys trying to say? That I shot a guy and made him jump off the bridge?"

"No, not at all. Look, Bruno, you're not in any trouble here," Jim said. "We just need to find out who the guy was. Get it?"

Bruno stood. "I need to take some Advil, my back's starting to act up again." He hustled out of the room and into the hall. "Be right back," he shouted.

I looked at Jim. "What's going on with this guy?"

"Not sure, but he looks scared."

"Of what? Some nut hops out of his cab and jumps off the bridge. It's not his fault."

"He had to stop on the bridge for that to happen. Why? Why did he stop?"

Before we had time to ponder the question, Bruno stepped back into the room. "I called my lawyer. He said not to talk to you guys anymore unless he's with me."

"Why do you have a lawyer? Have you been in trouble before?" Jim asked.

"No, never, he's my wife's brother. You guys will have to leave now."

Jim shook his head. "This looks bad for you, Bruno. Real bad."

Bruno stared at his shoes. "I know … but … but … you guys have to leave. Sorry."

When we got back into Jim's car, we both sat quietly staring out the front window. Then Jim said, "He's guilty."

I shook my head. "Of what?"

"I dunno … of somethin'."

CHAPTER TWELVE

J im dropped me in front of my building, but rather than go inside I fished through my pockets for the business card Josie had given me. The office for Hans Van den Brink, the guy who screwed her out of almost $10,000, was located at 237A Folsom Street, a block and a half from mine.

The building at 237 Folsom was a fancy high rise that housed multiple high powered financial institutions and investment banking firms. However, 237A Folsom was a door at the end of a short alley that ran parallel to the skyscraper. Under a peephole in the door was taped a handwritten placard: Van den Brink Investing. Call 415-555-2763 for entry.

I dialed the number and was greeted by an unfriendly voice. "Who are you?"

"I'd like to see Mr. Van den Brink," I replied.

"Why?"

"I was referred to him."

"By who?"

"The woman who owns the coffee truck on Harrison."

"Really? What did she say about him?"

"That even though she lost a little money with him,

she felt he had a lot of integrity."

"She said that?"

"Yeah."

"Was she sincere?"

"She sounded like it."

"Look up to your right and stand in front of the blinking blue light." I did as he asked and smiled at the camera. "Open your jacket and turn around." I did that also.

The lock clicked and a man with dyed hair that was probably once gray, but now a shade of orange, opened the door. "Sorry about the security measures, a lot of unsavory characters around here. I'm Hans Van den Brink."

I stepped into an office furnished with a beat-up desk, two folding chairs and a cot with a blanket and pillow strewn on top. "So, what can I do for you?" he asked.

"I hear you sell that computer money and stuff like that."

Van den Brink pulled out one of the metal chairs and slid it in my direction. "Please, sit. Apologies for the office, the new furniture hasn't arrived yet. I didn't get your name."

"Floyd, Floyd Percy."

"Nice to meet you, Floyd. So, you want to get into crypto, do you?"

"Yeah, that's it, crypto. You got any of it for sale?"

"Well, I'm just a broker. I'm the middleman between crypto exchanges and the consumer. What else did the coffee lady tell you?"

"She said you usually double people's investment in six months, but she was unlucky and hit a slump in the market."

He shook his head and forced a condescending smile. "I feel really bad about her loss, but of course I never promised her anything." He looked around as if to make sure no one was listening. "I shouldn't tell you this, but I have clients who have tripled their money in less time than that."

"Wow, that sounds great."

"How much were you interested in investing?"

I scratched the top of my head like it might stimulate some brain cells. "Not sure. My grandmother just passed and I guess I was her favorite 'cause a lot of cash will be coming my way real soon."

"Oh, sorry about grandma, but cash is perfect. I can get you a 10% discount for cash."

"Really? How do you do that?"

"Well, instead of going with the big outfits like Bitcoin or Ethereum, I use a firm called Cryptocrypt. They give brokers an extra 10% discount for cash and I pass it on to you."

I put on my happy face. "That's pretty generous of you."

"It's my pleasure to do it."

"But, hey, I heard banks will report it to the IRS if I withdraw over $10,000."

"So, you're thinking of investing more than that?"

"Yeah, around a hundred."

"Thousand?"

"Yeah, at least."

"Well, you're right about the banks. So, what I tell my big investors like you, is to only withdraw $9,900 per day. That way in ten days you're fully invested and we stay under the fed's radar."

I looked at Hans like he'd just come up with a new formula for quantum physics. "Smart." I stood to leave. "I'll be in touch as soon as I get the inheritance."

~ * ~

I thought it was a good idea to bring my boss up to speed on our new John Doe, so I took the elevator to the third floor and dropped in on Alex. Her corner office is what we call a three-holer. Two windows on one wall and a single on another.

The receptionist was on a break, so I knocked on her door and peeked in. "Good time?"

"Sure, come in." She pointed to a seat next to her desk.

"Thought I'd bring you up to speed on our John Doe," I said.

"All ears."

"First of all, the growth that you and I found was diagnosed as an Adenoid Cystic Carcinoma of the sublingual salivary gland."

She frowned. "I hate to admit it, but I've never heard of an ACC in that region."

"Neither have I, it's rare but not unheard of."

"How bad was it?"

"Terminal."

"You mean our guy was dying from cancer when he got shot and then jumped off the bridge?"

It was sad, but I couldn't help but laugh. "Talk about hitting the trifecta."

"Did Helmut think he was in radiation treatment?"

"He didn't think so. Actually, he suspects the guy wasn't in any treatment at all."

"Maybe he didn't know he had it."

"A lump that big under your tongue? Pretty hard to miss."

"It's worth checking the cancer centers, maybe you can ID him there."

"Already thought of that. I'll start on it this afternoon. But there's another strange development in the case."

"Strange?"

"Yeah, Jim and I tracked down the cab driver who let our guy off in the middle of the bridge. He denies having stopped and is scared to talk about it."

"That's good news, about finding him I mean. If you can get him to open up it might just solve the case for you.

"He's talking about getting a lawyer, which seems like overkill, if you'll excuse the pun."

"Keep me in the loop."

That was the signal to end the conversation. I stood to leave. "I will, of course."

Before I reached the door Alex said, "Oh, Rick, I owe you a birthday dinner, when would you like to collect?"

Two days ago, I would have leaped at a chance to have dinner with Alex. But after my date with Frankie, the torch I'd been carrying for Alex had begun to burn out. Even so, I couldn't be rude. "Anytime, my calendar's wide open."

"Okay, let's make it Friday evening. Should I send a limo?"

"Alex, it's not a funeral, it's a dinner, I'll grab an Uber and pick you up. Seven o'clock?"

"Perfect. Just give me a call when you're out front."

CHAPTER THIRTEEN

After almost four years searching for the identities of John Does, I've concluded that searching is usually not as hard as deciding where to search. This case was no exception. The jumper had mouth cancer. He must have known he had it, so it was likely, whether he treated it or not, that he had consulted with an oral surgeon, an ear nose and throat specialist, a hospital or a cancer center.

So, where do I start? I checked the most up-to date statistics for San Francisco. There were seventy-five oral and maxillofacial surgeons, one hundred and twenty-six ear nose and throat docs, twenty hospitals, and nine independent cancer centers.

I decided to play the numbers game. There were too many oral surgeons and ENTs to reasonably interview. Even twenty hospitals would be a strain on my resources. But nine cancer centers? That might be workable.

The Dillon Brady Comprehensive Cancer Center was at the top of my list. I dialed the number and as expected got a receptionist, and as I also expected she asked, "How may I direct your call?"

"This is Dr. Rose from the medical examiner's office. I need to speak with your director."

"Please hold."

I expected a collection of instrumental elevator music, but instead I was treated to an encyclopedia of the different cancers that are treated at the Center—not a pleasant list. After five minutes a human came online. "Janice Franklin."

"Yes, Ms. Franklin, this is Dr. Rose from the medical examiner's office. Are you the director?"

"No, sir, I'm the assistant to the director's assistant. How may I help you?"

"I was hoping to speak to the director about obtaining information on a patient."

"We don't give out information on patients. Those records are protected by HIPAA, the Health Insurance Portability and Accountability Act of 1996."

"This patient is dead, so I doubt HIPAA would apply."

"How long ago did the patient die?"

"About a week ago."

"I'm sorry, Doctor, you'll have to wait another forty-nine years and fifty-one weeks"

"Excuse me?

"The statute protects patient records for fifty years after death."

I grinned because I'd done my homework. "I believe there are HIPAA exceptions that allow the disclosure of protected health information in murder cases."

"Your patient was murdered?"

"Correct." There was silence on the other end of the line. "Are you still there?" I asked.

"Yes, please hold for the director's assistant."

After another lengthy description of treatment options, I heard a click. "Martha Winfield."

"Yes, Ms. Winfield, my name's Dr. Rose, I'm with the

medical examiner's office. I have a murder victim and need medical information on him."

"We can't provide that over the phone, Doctor, but if you could stop by with your credentials, I'll get permission to give you copies. What's the patient's name?"

"That's just it, I'm trying to establish identification for this victim."

"You don't know his name?"

"No, not yet."

"How do you know he was a patient here?"

"I don't."

"Well, Doctor, I can't look up records on a person with no name or any evidence that he was a patient here."

"Who at your clinic might be able to help me?"

"Only the director, Dr. Teeter."

"Oh, wow, I never thought of talking to the director. May I speak to him?"

"I'm afraid not. He's out of town until tomorrow."

I realized this approach wasn't working and decided not to waste my time on other clinics, at least until I could talk to the director of this one. I left my contact number, requested a call back, thanked the assistant, and hung up. Then, I headed over to the police station.

The sergeant standing guard over Mike Kelly's office announced my arrival and showed me in after getting the okay from the chief. Mike jumped out of his chair and met me at the door with a handshake and a pat on the back. "I hear you're doing a great job on that jumper case."

"You must have talked to my mother. I need help, Mike."

He pointed to a chair and I took a seat across from him. "Okay," he said. "What do you need?"

"You talk to Jim at all?"

"I did. He's the one who said you're doing a great job."

"So, you heard about our lawyered-up cab driver."

"Jim said he looked scared."

"He is scared. You know, Mike, he's the key to this case. We have to squeeze him."

"What are you thinking?"

"How about the Bullpen?"

"You really want this guy to sweat, don't you?"

"Look, he's hiding something, something big. He seems like a nice guy but yes, let him sweat a little."

"What about this lawyer he said he contacted?"

"Put him and his lawyer on one side of the table and you, Jim and me on the other. Last time I checked, three is a bigger number than two."

Mike laughed. "Damn, I might hire you for the department."

"No thanks, I'd rather work for a living."

"What, you think we sit around and drink coffee all day?"

"Not at all, sometimes you drink lattes."

Mike broke out laughing again. "Okay, I'll set up the interview. How far are you willing to go with this guy?"

"You're the cop. You decide."

CHAPTER FOURTEEN

S tella had been on my case lately for spending too much of my own money on Ubers and taxis, so this morning I hopped onto the cable car. Usually, I perched on the outside platform hanging onto a pole, but it was so foggy and damp I took one of the inside wood bench seats next to the gripman.

An hour later I was sitting at my desk playing today's Wordle when Stella's voice echoed through the intercom, "Captain Kelly's on line two."

I pushed the blinking button. "Mike, how's the interview appointment going?"

"That's what I'm calling about. Bruno's lawyer wants to do it this afternoon."

"Fine with me. How about Jim?"

"He's good. See you at my office at two?"

"I'll be there."

I had time to kill before the interview and figured it would be a good time to catch up with Stella's love life. She was running a spreadsheet on her computer when I sat down on the edge of her desk. "I hope you're not working on next year's budget."

She lifted her head out of the computer. "I was just running an estimate of how much you spend every year on taxis, Ubers and lattes."

I wasn't sure why Stella was on this mission to save me money, but I have to admit I was a little curious about her conclusions. "So, how much?"

"I have no idea what you spend on weekends. This is just Monday through Friday."

"Okay, how much?"

She ran her finger down the screen. "I don't know what cable cars cost, but one taxi a day for $15.00, five days a week for fifty weeks comes to $3,750. One Uber a day at $12.00, five days a week for fifty weeks is $3,000 and two lattes per day, including the generous tip you give Josie, is $20.00, times five, times fifty, totaling $5,000. You want to hear the bottom line?"

My curiosity had waned. "Actually no, but I guess you're going to tell me."

"$11,750."

"Okay, well, I have to get to and from work, so I guess the only place to cut the budget is with the lattes."

Stella furrowed her brows. "I was thinking you could take the bus."

"The bus? Last time I rode a bus was when I was in high school. No, I think I'll cut out the lattes."

"Well, since Ubers are cheaper than taxis, maybe just cut out the taxis."

"Cabbies need our support, but Josie can get by without our lattes."

Stella looked a little flustered. "You know, these numbers seem a little high. I think I'll run them again."

I hit the power button on her PC and the screen went black. "Forget it. I like taxis, I like Ubers, and I particularly like having lattes with you. So, as long as I can afford everything, the only thing I'm cancelling is my annual rectal exam."

"Really? Is it that expensive?"

"No, it's covered 100% on my medical insurance ... but I hate it."

She held onto a laugh as long as she could. "Damn it, Rick, you're messing with me."

"So, tell me, how's the romance with my favorite bartender going?"

"Maverick?"

"Are you dating any other bartender?"

"No. It's going good, except ..."

"Let me guess, he doesn't get off work until two in the morning."

"How did you know?"

"The bags under your eyes. Do you wait up every night?"

"Every night except Monday and Thursday. He's off those nights." She closed her eyes and put her head in her hands. "Rick, I can't take it anymore. What should I do?"

"How about a new boyfriend?"

"But, Maverick's so ... "

"... So cute, I know. Listen, you give me lovelorn advice, so I'll give you some. Cute wears off real fast, but exhaustion lasts forever. Unless you want to trade in your career for cocktail waitressing, your schedules will never mesh."

Stella stood and kissed me on the cheek. "Thanks. I knew that but I needed someone else to say it." She looked at her watch. "Can I buy you lunch? You need to save some money."

If ever I had a daughter, I'd want her to be just like Stella, but I knew it would never happen, so she's my surrogate—the closest I'll ever come. "I'd love that, but can you give me a raincheck? I have an appointment with

Captain Kelly."

~ * ~

There are several interview rooms at police head-quarters: The reception room for soft interviews, the captain's personal office where things get more heated, and then there's the Bullpen, when instead of an interview, there's an interrogation.

As one of the interrogators, I've been in the Bullpen several times and I can unequivocally say it's not a happy place. The walls are gray, the table and chairs are metal and the lighting is harsh. There are no windows other than the two-way glass one, so expertly depicted in every police drama on TV.

I was the last to arrive. On one side of the table sat Mike Kelly, Jim Allen and an empty chair—conspicuously reserved for me. On the other side sat Bruno Cappelletti, the last person to see the jumper alive, and next to him was his lawyer, a guy dressed in a faded blue suit and a stained lavender tie.

As soon as I took my seat, Mike Kelly opened the conversation. "Dr. Rose, you know everyone other than Mr. Cappelletti's counsel … Mr. Mancini." We looked at each other and nodded.

Mike turned on a tape recorder and said, "For the record let it be known it is September 6, 2023, at 14:27 hours. I am Mike Kelly, chief of homicide and I am joined by Detective Jim Allen of the SFPD and Dr. Rick Rose from the San Francisco medical examiner's office. Across the table from us is Mr. Bruno Cappelletti and his attorney, Enzo Mancini. Mr. Cappelletti, may I call you Bruno?"

Bruno, who was already sweating profusely, wiped his forehead with a stained handkerchief. "Sure, that's my name."

"Okay, Bruno, you told detective Allen and Dr. Rose that on the morning of August 22, 2023, at approximately 3:30 a.m. you drove a man in your taxi across the Golden Gate Bridge. Is that correct?"

"Yeah, that's right."

"Where did you pick up this man?"

"I told them guys. On the Embarcadero."

"And where did you take this man?"

"I already said. Sausalito."

"Where in Sausalito?"

"I dunno, just Sausalito."

"May I step in, Captain?" Jim asked.

Mike nodded and leaned back in his chair. Jim leaned forward in his. "Isn't it policy at your company to log in the location where you drop off a fare?"

Bruno looked at Mancini, hoping he would throw him a lifeline, but his lawyer didn't say a word. "Yeah, that's the policy."

"Why didn't you follow policy?"

"I did, I logged in Sausalito."

"So, if you were to take a fare to somewhere in Los Angeles, you'd only log Los Angeles as the destination?"

"No, I'd write down the exact location."

"So, why not in Sausalito?"

"I dunno. I was tired. I cut a corner. I go to jail for that?"

"No, Bruno, you don't go to jail for that. You go to jail for lying to the San Francisco police department. You are lying, aren't you?"

Bruno looked again at Mancini, who was still sitting mute. I felt sorry for the cabbie, his lawyer was obviously incompetent. "Enzo, help me out here," Bruno said.

This got his lawyer's attention. "My client wishes to

execute his fifth amendment rights and refuses to answer the question."

I wanted Bruno to tell us the truth about that night, but I couldn't stand by and let his attorney throw him under the fifth amendment bus. "Mr. Mancini," I said. "What specialty of the law do you practice?"

Now, he was starting to sweat too. "Personal injury, mainly. A little divorce stuff ... you know, only occasionally though."

"Have you ever handled a criminal case?"

"Well, no, but this isn't a criminal case."

I shook my head. "Mr. Mancini, you just made it one."

"How do you figure that?"

"The man in Bruno's cab jumped off the bridge, but he died of a gunshot wound. Our expert verified that at the morgue. If Bruno doesn't tell us what happened, these police officers are going to arrest him for being an accessory to murder."

"They are?"

"That's right," Mike Kelly said.

Perspiration rings were beginning to form under the armpits of Mancini's suit jacket. "Oh," he said. "Well, in that case I withdraw my fifth amendment thing." He looked at Bruno. "You better tell them."

All eyes turned to Bruno, who knew he'd just been abandoned. "I ... I can't," he said.

I leaned in towards him. "Look, if you didn't do anything wrong, you don't have anything to worry about."

"I want to help, I do, I just can't," he whimpered.

It was hard to believe this guy had anything to do with the jumper's death and I was all for letting him go. But Mike and Jim were career cops and they'd been through this type of scenario a hundred times. Jim took out a set of handcuffs. "Mr. Cappelletti, stretch out your hands, please."

Bruno set his hands on the table and Jim snapped the metal cuffs around his wrists. "Bruno Cappelletti," he said. "You're under arrest as an accessory to the murder of one John Doe. You have the right to remain silent ..."

I felt nauseous and stepped out of the room. A few minutes later Mancini came out and I looked at him with contempt. "Do you call yourself a lawyer?" I said.

He had a sheepish expression glued across his face. "Look, I'm doing my best, but I can't help him. Of all the people in that room, you're the only one who can."

"What do you mean?"

"Look, Bruno's a good guy and he didn't have anything to do with that man's death, but he's afraid of those cops. Maybe if you talk to him one on one, without those guys badgering him, he'll tell you what you need to know."

Enzo Mancini walked out the door and left me thinking that maybe he wasn't as incompetent as he seemed.

~ * ~

Despite Stella's spreadsheet presentation, I took a taxi home. After feeding Einstein, I had an urge for pasta, but I'd given up cooking for myself a year ago. Why bother if there's no one to share it with?

I checked out my supply of frozen dinners and vacillated between Marie Callender's Four Cheese Ravioli and Bertolli's Italian Sausage & Rigatoni. I knew my cardiologist wouldn't approve of either, but I chose the ravioli. That way I could tell him I'd cut down on my meat intake.

I parked on the couch and turned on the TV. It went straight to Netflix and I clicked on an old TV show named Quincy M.E.—a drama series about a medical examiner who solves John Doe cases. After the first episode I concluded it's much easier to be a medical examiner on TV than it is in real life. I finished the pasta and fell asleep.

CHAPTER FIFTEEN

As tired as I was, I couldn't stay asleep. My mind kept playing and replaying Enzo Mancini's words: "Maybe, if you talk to him one on one, without those guys badgering him, he'll tell you what you need to know." Finally, I drifted off but had one of those crazy dreams I often have, when I'm in the middle of a difficult case.

I'm in the back seat of a taxi and it's driving across the Golden Gate Bridge. In the middle of the span the cab stops and the driver turns around. It's Bruno; he has a frightening look on his face. "Get out," he says. I peer through the window, but all I see is fog. "Get out," he says again. I open the door. I step into the fog. I look back. "Well, jump, if you're going to," Bruno shouts. I approach the safety rail. I put one foot over the side. "Wait," he yells. I turn. I see him coming toward me. He's holding something. "You forgot this," he says. He hands it to me. I can't make out what it is. I reach for it. I lose my balance. I fall from the railing into the abyss. I woke up drenched in sweat.

I remember Frankie saying her seminars at Stanford start at 10:00 a.m. and she usually catches the 9:10 train to Palo Alto. I looked at my phone, it was 7:35. I tapped her number on my speed dial.

"*Allô*, Rick, is anything wrong?" she answered.

"No, not at all. Sorry for calling so early, but I wanted to reach you before you left for the train station. Any chance we could get together today for a professional consultation?"

There was silence on the other end of the phone. After a few seconds, she said, "Do you need therapy, Rick?"

I realized how stupid I must have sounded. "Well, I probably do, but I phrased that wrong. I'm working on a case and I need some expertise in psychology to move forward with it."

She laughed. "Oh, I understand, of course, I'll help anyway I can."

"I was hoping we could get together today, after you get back from Stanford. Would that work?"

"Yes, I have a short day today, so that would work very well. I could grab the 12:40 train back to San Francisco."

"Great, I'll meet you at the station and we'll get a bite nearby."

~ * ~

The Caltrain station is located at 4th and Townsend Streets, six blocks south of my office. Frankie's train was on time, but I couldn't pick her out of the crowd that flowed like a tsunami toward the exit.

As the mass of people thinned, I figured she must have missed the 12:40 and would probably be on the next train at 1:10. I turned to leave and felt a tap on my shoulder. "Leaving without me?"

At first, I didn't recognize her. The woman I had dinner with the other night was dressed to the nines.

This young lady was wearing distressed jeans, a Stanford sweatshirt and sneakers. To add to my confusion, her shoulder length hair was tied into a ponytail that stuck out from the back of a SF Giant's cap. I recovered quickly. "Sorry, miss, I think I'm waiting for your mother."

She rose up on the toes of her sneakers and kissed me on the cheek. "You've never seen my mother."

"I bet she's beautiful."

Frankie handed me a hardcover that weighed more than my cat. "Mind carrying a schoolgirl's book?"

"Will it get me another one of those French kisses?"

"We'll see. Depends on what kind of lunch you buy me."

MoMos, my favorite bar to not drink alcohol at, was only a three-block walk. As soon as we stepped through the front door, Maverick spotted us and pointed to the stools at the end of bar. While I placed Frankie's book on the bar and pushed her stool up close, Maverick set coasters and a ramekin of nuts in front of us. "Dr. Rose, the man with the prettiest girls in town. I know what you're not drinking, what can I get the lady?"

"Hey, Maverick, this is Dr. Barbier," I said. "She's a real doctor from France, not just a dentist from Brooklyn, so be careful what you say."

He gently lifted her hand and kissed it lightly. "*Bonjour, enchanté.*"

Frankie smiled and withdrew her hand. "If I were to answer in French, would you know what I said?"

Maverick laughed, "Hell, no, but it's still nice to meet you." He took our drink order and moved on.

"Why did you not include yourself as a real doctor?" Frankie asked.

"I don't know, I always felt the bar was set lower for

me than for the M.D.'s."

"Rick, Jacques has told me about the work you do. Your bar is much higher than you think."

I come from the old school where we were taught to show more interest in others than in ourselves. "How long is your fellowship?" I asked

"Did you just pivot?"

"Sort of. How long?"

"Just a year."

"Then?"

"I don't know, really. Maybe back to Paris, unless …?"

"Unless, what?"

"Unless there's a good reason to stay."

Before I could ask what a good reason might be, Maverick set down our drinks. "Chardonnay for the real doctor and an O'Doul's non-alky for the other doctor." He looked down at the book on the bar and read the title out loud. "*Diagnostic and Statistical Manual of Mental Disorders, Fifth Edition.*" He wrinkled his nose. "I liked the movie better." Frankie cracked up. I ordered a couple of burgers.

"So, other than wanting to spend hours in my company, tell me why you are buying me lunch?" she said.

"Okay, I have this cab driver who dropped his passenger off in the middle of the Golden Gate Bridge, so the guy could jump off. The driver says he never stopped on the bridge, but we know he did. If I'm ever going to ID the jumper, I need get the truth from the cabbie, but he's afraid to tell us the truth."

"Okay, so what's the question?"

"I'm going to interview the cab driver by myself, without the cops around. They scare him. I'm not sure how to get him to open up …"

"So, you are seeking interrogation techniques?"

"No, sorry, that's not it. I know this sounds weird, but last night I had a dream that I was the guy in the cab who dove off the bridge and just before I took the leap, the driver wanted to give me something I'd left in the cab. As hard as I tried, I couldn't make out what it was. Why would I dream that?"

"Maybe, the jumper did leave something in the cab before he got out."

"But how would I know that? How could I dream about something I have no knowledge of?"

"People give off subliminal messages. Maybe the cab driver gave one to you."

"I get that advertisers can design subliminal messages to make me buy potato chips, but this guy isn't that sophisticated."

"Look, Rick, this is just a theory and I may be way off base here, but subliminal messages are stimuli presented below a person's threshold of conscious awareness, with the intention of influencing their thoughts, feelings, or behaviors. This cab driver may have given you a subliminal message without even realizing he was doing it."

This was heady stuff they didn't teach in dental school. "So, when I interview him, how do I get the truth out of him?"

"You know, Rick, if he actually sent you a message that he's not aware he sent, you're going to have to probe to bring it to the surface."

"How?"

"Go on the assumption that your dream was based on something real. Not exactly in its real form, but still real. Keep building trust with this guy until he finally lets it out. He'll be grateful. It's like holding an upset stomach until you can't hold it anymore and the feeling of relief after you purge it."

The food arrived. "You know something, Frankie?" I asked.

"What?"

"You are the difference between a real doctor and the other doctor."

She looked at me and shook her head. "No, Rick, I'm not. You are one of the real doctors too. Show me a psychiatrist who could do the job you are doing."

CHAPTER SIXTEEN

A fter talking to Enzo Mancini, Bruno's brother-in-law / lawyer, and Dr. Francoise Barbier, my dinner date and psychiatrist, I knew I had to talk to Bruno alone. It had been almost twenty-four hours since he was arrested and I wasn't sure if Mike Kelly still had him in custody. There was only one way to find out.

"Captain Kelly," he answered.

"Mike, it's Rick."

"Oh, hey, Rick, I didn't look at the ID. You calling about our cab driver detainee?"

"Yeah, you still holding him?"

"We're letting him out in two hours. Do you want us to take another crack at him before that?"

"No. Listen, Mike, I want to talk to him one on one—no cops."

"Changing tactics?"

"I think so. He's too scared to talk to you guys and his lawyer thinks he may trust me."

"I don't know if I'd trust his lawyer."

"I know, I get it. He's an ambulance chaser, but he is Bruno's brother-in-law and he knows Bruno. I'm going to trust him on this."

"Okay, our guy will be out of here by noon. After that

he's all yours."

~ * ~

I didn't expect a return call from the director of the Dillon Brady Comprehensive Cancer Center and I was correct. I looked up their address and found they were located at the corner of Divisadero and Geary, not far from the old Mt. Zion Hospital. Uber charged me $12.80. Stella would be happy; I charged it to the office account.

I'd never been inside a cancer center and was expecting a bleak atmosphere. As I often am, I was one hundred percent wrong. As soon as I entered, I could sense an upbeat and positive feeling. The walls were papered in shades of orange and pink, pictures of smiling faces hung everywhere, and the music that piped through the speakers had a beat that made me want to tap my foot.

The receptionist reminded me of Stella—bouncy, happy and engaging. "Hi," she said. "And welcome. Are you new to our center?"

"Well, yes, but I'm not a patient."

"No problem, how may I help?" I handed her my card and wasn't surprised by her reaction. "Odontologist? Oh, you straighten teeth."

I've been doing this job for four years and almost everyone who reads my card has the same response. I used to explain that I'm a forensic dentist, totally different from an orthodontist, but I gave up on that a year ago. "Yes, and I can see your teeth are perfect."

"Thank you, Doctor. I just finished with two years of Invisalign. So, what can I do for you?"

"I need to talk to the director, Dr. Teeter."

"Is he expecting you, Dr. Rose?"

"Not really. I spoke with his assistant a couple of days ago."

She smiled her infectious smile and checked a sheet that I could see had a long list of names. "I'm supposed to put walk-ins on the bottom of the list, but I'm going to sneak you in next. Can I get you something while you wait? Coffee, tea, juice?"

"No, thanks. But, if you ever need help with your Invisalign, make sure to give me a call."

After my previous phone conversation, where I had to go through the director's assistant's assistant, and then his actual assistant, I was expecting a similar process for my in person visit—wrong again. A nicely dressed woman escorted me from the reception room straight to the director's office.

A slightly overweight man with a short gray beard and temples to match stood to greet me with an outstretched hand. "Dr. Rose ... Ralph Teeter. Please have a seat." We sat across from each other in cushioned chairs near a glass-top coffee table. "I must apologize, Dr. Rose, my assistant passed on your message and I've been meaning to call you, but I got swamped and ..."

"Call me Rick, please. And no apology necessary, I've been there myself."

"Interesting profession, forensic odontology, how did you make that career choice?"

"It's a long story. Suffice it to say, circumstances made the choice for me."

"Well, you appear to be doing well at it. I've read about several of your cases in the morning *Chronicle*."

I was impressed. It's not often you can show up unannounced and interrupt a man's busy schedule and then have him dole out a compliment to start the conversation. "Thanks, Ralph," I said. "I didn't think anyone read that stuff."

"Some of us do. So, Rick, how can I help you?"

"I have a John Doe in the morgue who needs a name. As part of the autopsy, I found a growth which turned out to be a salivary gland adenoid cystic carcinoma."

"Parotid?"

"No, sublingual."

"My, that's rare."

"That's why I'm here. I don't think it was ever treated, but I'm hoping he at least consulted with a specialist or a treatment center."

"I try to stay up to date on our cases and I think I would have remembered an ACC of the sublingual salivary gland, but I'm more than happy to check the database for you."

"I'd appreciate that."

Dr. Teeter went to his desk and began tapping the keys of his computer. After a five-minute finger exercise, he called me over. "Take a look, only one ACC in the last twelve months and it was a parotid gland."

I knew it was a longshot and wasn't surprised I'd struck out. "Any idea where I should go next? I can't interview every cancer center, hospital, ENT and oral surgeon in San Francisco."

He rubbed his chin while he thought. "Tell you what, there's a Head and Neck Cancer Conference coming up at the Moscone Center in a couple of days. I'll circulate the word. There's a chance, albeit a small one, it will ring a bell. Like I said, an ACC of the sublingual gland is something most people in the field would remember. It's worth a try. I'll be in touch."

~ * ~

When I got back to my office I took the elevator to the basement. I hadn't been to the morgue since Alex and

I performed the exam on John Doe's mouth. Nothing had changed. The smell was intolerable. Beethoven's 5th was blaring through the speakers and Helmut was skimming through a book twice the size of a Bible. He looked up when I stepped through the door. "Hey, Rick, where have you been? I haven't seen you in a week."

"Yeah, sorry, this case is swallowing me up. I was wondering what your ballistics guy had to say about the bullet that killed the jumper."

"Oh, yeah, I didn't call you because he's still working on it."

"Still? How long does it take to ID a bullet?"

"Not long, usually, except it seems our guy wasn't shot with your everyday weapon."

"I don't get it. What d'ya mean?"

"Well, he knows the bullet is a 9mm, but he can't identify the make or model of the gun."

"Are there that many guns that shoot 9mm bullets?"

"Absolutely, 9mm is the most common handgun size on the market."

"Huh, any idea how long before he can pin it down?"

He shrugged. "I'll keep bugging him, shouldn't be too long."

I wasn't really sure if the information would be of any help to me and I knew I had no control over some guy in a ballistics lab, so I thanked Helmut and left for the day.

CHAPTER SEVENTEEN

I f I called on the phone, I had a pretty good hunch Bruno wouldn't talk to me. So, after my breakfast oatmeal I contacted White Cab, said I was Bruno's brother-in-law and asked if he was working this morning. I was told he was scheduled to drive the graveyard shift tonight.

In San Francisco you know you're getting close to Ocean Beach, when you breathe in the smell of the seawater. Bruno's home is located on the corner of 47th and Noriega, where you can't mistake the salty air.

When Josie and I were first married, we looked at a 1400 sq. ft. home in the area. The realtor told us that when it was built, back in the 1940s, it sold for a whopping $5,000. When we looked at it, in 2014, it was around $600,000. Knowing the surge in San Francisco house prices, it's probably worth a lot more now. For his sake, I hoped Bruno bought it a long time ago.

I knocked on the door and a woman wearing a house dress covered by a checkered apron, opened it. Bruno must have described me to her because the first words out of her mouth were, "Go away."

The door began to close and I wedged my shoe between it and the jamb. "Please, Mrs. Cappelletti, I want to help Bruno."

"He doesn't need your help."

"I'm not a policeman. Tell him Dr. Rose needs to speak to him."

She kicked my ankle and I pulled it away from the door. "Wait," she said and slammed it in my face.

I could hear voices arguing inside, most likely about whether to let me in or not. After about five minutes and the sound of several slamming doors, Bruno opened the front one. "Come in," he said.

He led me to the living room and gestured toward an overused velour couch. "What d'ya want from me?" he asked.

"Look, Bruno, the point of my job is a simple one. I must make sure every person has a name before we bury them. You can help me find one of those names."

Bruno stared at his shoes, avoiding eye contact of any kind. "So, the guy in my cab, he's got no name?"

"He has one, everyone does, we just don't know what it is. Will you help me find it?"

"Listen, Doc, I want to help but .... but ..."

"Tell me, Bruno. Explain to me why you can't help me."

"I'm afraid."

"Of what?"

"I'm not a rich man, Dr. Rose. If I get in trouble over this and lose my medallion, my job, or go to jail, my family will be destroyed."

"Bruno, that's the last thing I would want to happen. I can help you, I know I can, but I need to know the truth. Can you tell me anything? Maybe just start with where you picked the guy up."

"I already told you and that a-hole cop, Allen."

"You said you picked him up on the Embarcadero. That's a long boulevard. Where on the Embarcadero?" Bruno lifted his gaze from his shoes and looked at me. I could see in his eyes he was struggling. "Just start there," I said. "If it doesn't feel right, then stop. I'm not going to make you tell me anything you don't want to tell me."

While he was thinking about my words, his wife stepped into the living room carrying a tray. "I have espresso and biscotti." She set the tray on the table. "You take sugar?" she asked me.

"Two, please." She dropped a couple of cubes into my cup and another into her husband's. "Would you like to join us?" I asked. She shook her head and left the room.

Bruno and I sat, sipping espresso, nibbling a biscotti, and saying nothing. When our cups were empty, he said, "Wharf Landing, across from Pier 39."

I wanted to start taking notes, but I knew that would make this conversation look like an interrogation; I decided to do my best to put it to memory. "Wharf Landing, is that an apartment house?"

"Condominiums. Expensive ones."

"So, our guy was just out front looking for a cab at three in the morning?"

"No, I saw an attendant open the door. Ya know, when ya drive a cab for twenty-six years, ya can smell a fare comin' your way, especially at three in the morning. I backed up and turned the light on in the cab."

"Then what?"

"A guy comes hobbling toward me and gets in the back seat."

"Hobbling? So, was he hurt? Could you tell he'd been shot?"

"I had no reason to think that. I didn't see any blood

on him."

"Was he wearing a jacket?"

"Yeah, a heavy one, like a ski parka."

"Maybe that's why you didn't see any blood."

"I dunno, maybe."

"So, where did he ask you to take him?"

"Well, at first he just wanted to get away from there, but he seen the Golden Gate up ahead and said he wanted to go to Sausalito."

Bruno was beginning to sweat, like he did at the police station and I didn't want him to draw a false equivalence between our talk and the interrogation he'd gone through. "You want to take a little break?" I asked.

"Yeah, yeah, I do. It's okay?"

I nodded. "Sure, of course. Bruno, I'm not a cop. Remember that."

He left the room and I could hear voices coming from the kitchen. There was no arguing like there had been before I was let into the house. This time, Mrs. Cappelletti was whimpering. It was painful for me to hear, but nowhere near the pain that those two must be feeling. "Why?" I whispered to myself,

In about ten minutes Bruno came back into the living room and flopped onto the couch. "Ya wanna hear more?"

"Do you want to tell me more?"

"Yeah, I do," he said, and he began tapping his foot up and down against the floor. "Anyway, this guy, he wasn't looking so good and he asks me for a towel. I thought maybe he was gonna puke in my cab. But he says, no, he just spilled champagne, or somethin' like that, on his shirt at a party he just left."

"So, you gave him the towel?"

"Yeah, and through the rearview mirror I saw him

stuff it under his jacket. You said he was shot, so I guess that's what the towel was for."

"What happened next?"

"Well, it was gettin' real foggy outside and I slowed up 'cause I had a little trouble seein' the approach lane. But once I got on the bridge I stepped on the gas."

"And?"

"He asked … no … he told me to slow up."

"Did he say why?"

"Nah, I just figured he was nervous that I was driving too fast in the fog."

"Then what?"

Bruno was quiet. I knew he was close to the midspan of the bridge, the part of the story where he said he didn't stop. I reconciled with the possibility that Bruno might not change his story and it would end, not here, but in Sausalito. Then Bruno said, "He put a gun through the privacy window and told me to stop."

I could feel the adrenaline shooting into my veins and felt my heart rate go off the charts. "Did you?" I asked.

"Hey, I got a family. Yeah, I stopped."

"And what did he do?"

"You know what he did. He jumped off the bridge."

"What about the gun?"

"What about it?"

"Did he take it with him?"

"I guess he did."

"So, that's it?"

"What more d'ya want. I told ya, he jumped."

"So, Bruno, why did you keep telling us that you didn't stop on the bridge?"

"I dunno, scared they'd take away my taxi medallion, I guess."

Something didn't add up. Sure, Bruno might have been afraid he would lose his medallion, but wouldn't that be better than being involved in a murder, or going to jail and not being able to support his family? No, this definitely did not add up. Then it struck me—my dream and Frankie's theory that Bruno may have sent me some sort of subliminal vibe.

"You never told me the jumper was carrying something. What was it?" I asked.

The color drained from Bruno's face. "What d'ya mean? Carrying somethin'?"

"When he got into your cab, he was carrying something, wasn't he?"

"No, nothin'."

"So, did he pay you for the ride or just stiff you?"

"He paid. Gave me forty bucks."

"Where did he get it?"

"I don't know, I guess he earned it."

"No, I mean where did he take the forty dollars from to pay you? Did he have a wallet, a purse, a clip, a case? He must have taken it out of something?"

"I dunno where he took it from. What's it matter? The guy was a wacko. He jumped off the friggin Golden Gate Bridge, for God's sake."

I sensed the hostility creeping into Bruno's voice, so I slowed up and spoke more quietly. "You're right, this guy must have had a lot of problems."

"Ya think?"

"Look, Bruno, this is important. I think the guy was carrying something, something he left behind in your cab. Do you remember what it was?"

His face was stoic and he rose from his chair. My first thought was that the conversation might be over, but I was wrong. "I'll be back," he said. He left the room and muted voices came from the kitchen once again.

In less than five minutes Bruno returned, and this time he was accompanied by his wife. They huddled together in an oversized chair and Mrs. Cappelletti spoke first. "My Bruno, if he tells you something, will you keep it a secret?"

How do I answer this question? What if Bruno shot the guy? What if he pushed him off the bridge? What if, what if? I had to trust my instincts. "Yes, Mrs. Cappelletti," I said. "I'll keep it a secret." She looked at her husband and nodded.

"He was carrying a leather briefcase," Bruno said.

"It wasn't found in the water. He left it in your cab, didn't he?"

Bruno looked down at his shoes again and whispered, "Yeah, he did."

"Why were you afraid to tell us?"

"'Cause he gave it to me, before he jumped."

"I'm not sure I get this. What was in the case?"

Bruno looked at his wife and she nodded again. "Two hundred and fifty thousand in cash," Bruno said.

I tried not to look shocked, but I doubt I was successful. "So, you kept the money?"

Mrs. Cappelletti, who had hardly spoken, stepped back into the conversation. "Dr. Rose, we have two daughters: Rosa, she's in college at Cal Poly, and Lucia, she's starting U.C. Berkeley in the fall. Do you know how much that costs each year?"

I had a pretty good idea, but I didn't want to guess. "No," I said.

"$39,700 for tuition, another $41,000 for room, board and books and $10,000 for incidental living expenses."

I did the quick math. "About $90,000. That's a lot of money."

"Bruno works double shifts and still only makes $75,000 a year, so we applied for a third mortgage on our house, which we knew we couldn't afford. Then, that man, the one who jumped, he gave Bruno this money. 'For your kids' college,' he said to Bruno."

I looked at Bruno. "Did he say anything else?"

"Yeah, he said 'be careful.' I'm not sure what that meant, but I figured it meant not to tell anybody. Dr. Rose, are you going to take it away from us?"

I'd already made a commitment to these people, when I promised not to reveal this conversation. "No, Bruno, I'm not." I stood to leave. "Thank you, both of you." I looked at Bruno. He was wiping tears from his eyes.

CHAPTER EIGHTEEN

T he first thing I did when I returned to my office was to google Wharf Landing - San Francisco: *A six story, twenty-five-unit condominium complex, located at the intersection of Beach Street and the Embarcadero, overlooking the San Francisco Bay waterfront. Construction began in February 2022 and was completed in May 2023. It is now among the costliest housing in the city, the last unit selling for $1,975 per square foot ...*

I knew I had to somehow check out Wharf Landing and I knew my only option was to have a badge with me when I did it. That meant I would have to ask Jim Allen or Mike Kelly to accompany me. It was way below Mike's pay grade, so that left Jim.

I had a good relationship with Jim; he was honest with me and I was honest with him. So, I was facing my first dilemma with this case. Jim would want to know how I got the lead on Wharf Landing and I would have to tell him it came from Bruno Cappelletti. But to keep the promise I made to the Cappellettis and keep secret the money given to Bruno by the jumper, I would have to lie to Jim.

I wanted to get my story straight before calling him and I spent an hour creating a scenario of truths and half-truths, all while a line of poetry echoed through my brain: *'Oh, what a tangled web we weave, when first we practice to deceive.'* I hoped it wouldn't apply to me.

Jim picked me up in his police-issue sports car, the black 4-door Chevy sedan. "So, why all the mystery on the phone?" he asked.

"No big mystery, I interviewed Bruno, that's all."

His eyes gave away his surprise. "He actually talked to you?"

"Yeah, his lawyer told me he was intimidated by you and Mike and thought I'd have better luck going it alone."

"Get anything?"

"He admitted he stopped on the bridge and let the guy out."

"Really? Why'd he lie to us about it?"

"He was afraid of losing his taxi medallion."

"Then why'd he stop?"

"The guy in the back seat pointed a gun at him."

"No shit? Did he pay for the cab ride?"

"Forty bucks."

Jim digested the information before coming to the same conclusion that I'd come to earlier. "He didn't have a wallet or money clip on him. Where'd he get the cash?"

"I asked Bruno that. He said the guy pulled two twenties out of his pocket and passed them through the window before he headed for the railing."

"That sounds like he had the suicide all planned—no ID, just forty bucks."

"Sounds that way."

"What about the gunshot wound? He didn't plan that."

"That's the mystery we have to figure out," I said.

"Any idea how?"

"Bruno gave me the name of the place where he picked our guy up. You familiar with a complex named Wharf Landing?"

He smirked. "In my dreams. A guy told me, if you had to ask the price of those condos, you couldn't afford one."

"Well, that's where we're headed."

~ * ~

Jim parked in the loading zone next to the front doors and we approached the uniformed doorman. Before he could ask what we needed, Jim opened his wallet and flashed his badge. "SFPD," he said.

The attendant was surprised but not intimidated. "Help you, sir?"

"Yeah, I think you can," Jim said. "You ever work the night shift?"

"No, I'm a family man, I leave that up to Sam."

"What's Sam's last name?

"Woodruff, Sam Woodruff."

"So, what time does Sam come on duty?"

"Seven tonight."

"How long's the shift?"

"We each do twelve hours."

"Any days off?"

"Monday and Tuesday."

"Who works those days?"

"A couple part time guys on social security, trying to make a few extra bucks."

Jim looked my way. "It was a Friday night," I said.

"So, who can give us Sam's contact information?" Jim asked.

"That would be the manager, Ms. Vargas."

"She have a first name?"

"I think it's Angela or Andrea … something like that."

He opened one of the doors and pointed toward a rotunda. "I just saw her go into her office."

The rotunda was beyond extravagant, it was opulent. The floor, a combination of black and white marble, met a circular wall painted in the faux style. And from the ceiling of a two-story dome, covered in what looked like gold leaf, hung an enormous crystal chandelier. Only five doors opened onto the rotunda. They read: Gentlemen, Ladies, Elevator, Stairs, and Managing Director.

We chose the fifth and were greeted by a well-dressed, well-manicured secretary. Jim went through his badge routine and asked to speak to the director. We were shown in immediately.

A striking woman dressed in a chic pantsuit, rose from her desk. "Gentlemen … Adriana Vargas."

"Detective Allen, SFPD," Jim said. He nodded toward me, "Dr. Rose from the San Francisco medical examiner's office."

She pointed to a small conference table. "Please, have a seat. Coffee, tea, a glass of wine perhaps?"

Jim shook his head. "No thanks, ma'am, we're just here to ask a few questions."

She sat down directly across from us. "As you wish. What can I help you with?"

I cut right to the chase. "Ms. Vargas, we believe a man was shot in this building during the early hours of August 22nd."

Her jaw didn't fall open, but it looked like it might. "That's preposterous. Are you sure you have the right building?"

"Quite sure."

"That was almost two weeks ago. Why would the police not have contacted me earlier?"

"The building wasn't identified until this morning, ma'am," Jim said.

She shook her head in disbelief. "That doesn't say much for our police department, does it now, Detective Allen? Was this man badly hurt?"

"He's dead, Ms. Vargas, that's why I'm here," I said.

"And, in which unit did this shooting take place?"

"That's what we're here to find out."

She made no effort to mask her indignation. "You claim a man was shot dead in this building, but you don't know where in this building?"

"He wasn't shot dead in this building, he was just shot. He died later, somewhere else."

Adriana Vargas stood, the universal signal for the end of a meeting. I continued to sit and so did Jim. She reluctantly sat back down. "What do you gentlemen want of me?" she asked.

"The names and contact information of all the owners in Wharf Landing and the contact information of the night doorman," Jim said.

"I can give you the doorman's information, but Detective Allen, please, you know I can't give out personal information about our owners without a court order of some sort."

Jim stood and I followed. "Fine," he said. "Give us what you can and we'll get a warrant from the judge for the rest. But, you realize, Ms. Vargas, that the warrant may cover the search of every unit in Wharf Landing."

Adriana Vargas' demeanor changed on a dime. "Detective Allen, I think I can get you what you want but give me a little time to discuss it with my board."

Jim handed her his card. "No problem, we'll give you thirty-six hours."

CHAPTER NINETEEN

Alex took care of the reservation but wouldn't tell me where she was taking me for my birthday dinner. My only responsibility was to pick her up at seven. I have a house at the bottom of Russian Hill and she owns an apartment in Pacific Heights. As the crow flies, we live about a mile apart apart, as the Uber drives, it's over two. I clicked the app.

We pulled up to her apartment, I gave her a call and two minutes later she stepped out the front door. Alex always looks good when she's at the office, but tonight she wasn't at the office and she looked magnificent. She was wearing a purple sheath with a black blazer and matching heels, a perfect complement to her green eyes.

I hopped out of the car to hold the door. "You look great," I said.

She smiled, "Thanks, so do you."

I rarely wear a tie. As a matter of fact, the last time I remember was at my wedding ten years ago. I wasn't about to dig that suit out of mothballs, so yesterday I stopped by Wilkes Bashford and picked up an outfit. "Just something I dragged out of the closet," I said. "So, where are we headed?"

"Ever been to Quince?"

I'd heard about Quince. It garnered a Michelin 3-star a couple years ago and was still one of the city's top restaurants. Unfortunately, it was also one of the priciest and out of range for what I would ever spend on a meal. "Yeah, love their big Quince McBurger," I said. "Especially with their curly fries."

Alex grinned and shook her head. "Are you ever serious?"

"I was, when I said you look great."

The place was elegant. It turns out their high-end meal is a prix-fixe, ten-course tasting event that features unique dishes paired with exotic wines at a price slightly higher than the monthly mortgage payment on my first house. Alex, knowing I don't drink, arranged for a table in the salon, where we were able to order ala carte without the fancy wines.

"How does the menu look?" Alex asked.

"Expensive."

"It's your fortieth birthday."

"Still expensive."

"If it makes you happy, I'll charge it to the office— write it off as entertaining a client."

"All our clients are dead."

"Will you please just order? I make a lot of money and believe me, I can afford this place."

"Well, since you put it that way, I'll start with the Tomales Bay oysters and get the Porcini mushroom tortellini for my main."

Alex started with the Tsar Nicoulai caviar and when it arrived along with my oysters, so did a bottle of sparkling wine. "Don't worry," she said. "It's Chateau De Fleur —non-alcoholic." She held up her glass. "Welcome to the fifth decade."

By now I was feeling like a jerk for making such a big deal about the prices and I tapped my glass to hers. "Thanks, Alex, I really appreciate this. You're not only a good boss, you're also a good friend."

During the middle of our main course I asked, "Mind if I talk a little shop?"

"So, you do want me to write off this dinner."

"No, that's not it. I have a problem I need help with."

"Go for it."

"I interviewed Bruno, the cab driver, and he opened up to me. He told me where he picked up the jumper and why he stopped to let him out in the middle of the bridge."

"That doesn't sound like a problem to me."

"That's not the problem part. He and his wife are keeping a secret and to find out what it is, I promised I would keep it a secret also."

"I still don't get the problem."

"Well, I'm not sure, but they may have committed a crime, so I can't discuss it with Jim or Mike, and to make matters worse I lied to Jim in order to keep my promise to Bruno and his wife."

"So, if a crime was committed, you could be guilty of being an 'accessory after the fact.'"

"If a crime was committed … but, I'm not sure it was."

The waiter passed our table and Alex summoned him over. "Could you bring me a double cognac?" He nodded and moved on.

I winced. "That bad, huh?"

"I'm not sure. I don't know the secret, and I assume you're not going to tell me, because if you do and I keep it a secret, I may be an accessory."

"Bingo."

Alex's drink arrived and rather than taking a sip she

took a gulp. "Tell you what, as much as I want to know, keep it to yourself for now. Normally, when the medical examiner's office has a legal problem I call the City Attorney, but he's also the attorney for the police department and I don't want you to get thrown under the bus. I'm going to have you meet with our independent counsel, who doesn't have any conflict of interest issues."

I shook my head. "Alex, I don't want to drag you or your budget into this. I'm the one who created the problem; I'll get my own lawyer."

"No, you won't. Look, Rick, you did what you thought was right, while trying to solve a case for me. It's my job to make sure you're protected and the budget has nothing to do with it."

The first time I met Alex, I thought she was a woman of high ethics and solid integrity, but thinking is not knowing. Now I knew. If she weren't my boss, I'd jump across the table and kiss her. Unfortunately, she was.

CHAPTER TWENTY

I knew I needed more exercise and Stella was pushing me to save money on transportation, so instead of taking a cab or Uber to work, I hopped on the cable car. It let me off at Powell and Market, which meant a six-block walk to my office. It made sense, no tipping drivers and no gym membership fees.

I set a latte in front of Stella. "Guess what?" I said.

"You bought me a new Corvette."

"Close. I took the cable car to work. Saved four bucks."

"I'm proud of you. Where are you going to put the savings?"

"In the coke machine, most likely. Any calls?"

"Your buddy, Jim Allen."

"He's not my buddy, he's a colleague. Okay?"

"Whatever he is, he gives me the heebie-jeebies."

"Why?"

"He's a letch. Whenever he's around me I can feel his eyes slithering all over my body. Doesn't he have a girlfriend or someone else to ogle?"

"I'll talk to him about it. Why did he call?"

"Something about a rough landing."

"Wharf Landing?"

"That's it. He said to call him back."

I picked up my cup, excused myself from the coffee klatch, and went into my private office. Jim's number was on my speed dial.

"Allen," he answered.

"Jim ... Rick ... what's up?"

"You'll never guess who I got a fax from."

It wasn't exactly a question for Jeopardy. "Adriana Vargas," I said.

"Man, you should be a contestant on ..."

"... Jeopardy, I know. Did she send the list?"

"Yeah, I'll bring it right over and we'll check it out."

I'd no sooner hung up, when my cell buzzed. I didn't recognize the number but answered it anyway. "Dr. Rose."

"Rick ... Ralph Teeter, from the cancer center."

"Oh, Dr. Teeter, hi, I didn't expect a call so soon."

"The conference I told you about started yesterday and I spread the word about that salivary gland ACC."

"And?"

"An ENT guy from UCSF hospital said he diagnosed one about three months ago."

"Did he treat the patient?"

"I didn't get into that. You have a pen handy?"

"Shoot."

"Dr. Eduardo Pérez. Otolaryngology is on the fifth floor."

"Thanks, Doc, I appreciate it."

"Please, just Ralph. Good luck, Rick."

The intercom buzzed and Stella's voice quivered, "Save me. Please."

I opened the door and saw Jim sitting on the edge of Stella's desk. She had her chair slid back as far as it would go and she heaved a sigh of relief when she saw me. "Jim, come on in," I said.

We sat down at a small table I'd commandeered from the building's storage closet and I decided to get Stella's problem out of the way before we got down to business. "Jim, you have to cut out that shit with my secretary."

His eyes opened wide like a monkey had just jumped down from the ceiling. "What?"

"You know what, stop invading her space and stop undressing her in your brain."

"Who? Me?"

"Yeah, you. Just cut it out, okay?"

"Hey, I'm a hot, testosterone filled, young stud."

"No, you're a lukewarm, alcohol saturated, middle-aged man."

I'd witnessed Jim, when someone pissed him off. I wasn't sure if I just had. I shut up and waited. "Can't blame a guy for tryin'," he laughed. "So, let's look at this list."

The fax was four pages long and identified the names of twenty-four owners. The only personal information included was one contact phone number for each owner. "What do we do?" I asked. "Call each one and ask if they shot a guy on August 22nd?"

"Good question. Let's see if any of these names ring a bell."

I ran my finger down the list of names on the first page and shook my head. Jim did the same. The second page was a repeat of the first. When we pulled up the third, a name jumped out at me. I pointed to it. "Recognize that guy?" I asked.

Jim peered down. "Yeah, the grifter you asked me to check out."

"Hans Van den Brink. How the hell can he afford a six-million-dollar condo?"

"Maybe he made a big score."

"I went to his office, the guy sleeps there and can't even afford a decent desk."

"You went to his office? Why?"

"I don't know. I guess I wanted to meet the asshole who would con a hard-working woman out of almost ten-thousand dollars."

"And?"

"He's small time. Sells phony crypto and keeps everything under ten grand so the IRS won't get nosey."

"Hey, con a hundred marks for ten thousand each and it equals a million—tax free."

"Still not enough for Wharf Landing. Are you thinking what I'm thinking?"

"My car's outside. Let's go."

~ * ~

The alley next to the high-rise looked even scruffier than the first time I was there. Someone must have spent the night and left behind half a pound of trash, which Van den Brink wasn't interested in picking up. I dialed the phone number on the handmade sign and looked up at the camera.

A voice on the other end said, "Floyd? Floyd Percy? I wasn't sure you'd be coming back. Who's that with you?"

"My financial advisor."

"Oh ... uh, okay... have him take off his coat and step closer to the camera." Jim stripped off his wind breaker and smiled at the blinking blue light. The door opened. "Come in, come in, so you brought an advisor, did you?"

"Yeah, Mr. Van den Brink, this is Jim Allen."

A glad hand sprung from Hans' pocket and continued in Jim's direction. "Call me Hans. So, you with a firm here in the city?"

Jim forced a smile. "Yeah, a big one."

"Schwab, Fidelity, Morgan Stanley …?"

Jim opened his wallet and held it in front of Hans. "San Francisco Police Department."

The color washed from Hans' face like turpentine dissolving paint. "I … I don't get it," he said. He looked at me. "Floyd, this is a joke, right?"

I shook my head. "Name's not Floyd, it's Rick, Rick Rose. My ex-wife owns the coffee truck on Harrison."

Hans began connecting the dots and it didn't take long to arrange them. "Hey, look, Floyd … Rick, I'm sorry your ex's investment didn't work out. Maybe we can talk about some reimbursement for her. We don't need to bring in the bunco squad."

"A reimbursement would be nice, but before we talk about that, we want to know how you can afford a condo in Wharf Landing."

He didn't see this coming and it showed. "What? What's that got to do with your ex-wife?"

"It has nothing to do with her," Jim said. "But how 'bout you answer Rick's question anyway."

Hans is a con man and when a con man knows his con won't work, he gets aggressive. "Tell you what, Mr. Detective, you can kiss my ass." He opened his cell phone. "I'm calling my lawyer."

Jim leaned over, took the phone from his hand, and tapped the red dot on the screen. "Not a good idea, Hans."

"And why is that?"

"I'm not here to arrest you … not yet anyway."

"Then what do you want, besides the coffee lady's money?"

"Like Rick said, we want to know how you can afford Wharf Landing."

"Why would I tell you that?"

"Because I asked and because I have a badge."

"How do I know I can trust you?"

"You don't, but I'm the only guy between you and a jail cell."

"If ... if I tell you, I might incriminate myself."

"If you don't, I'll arrest you."

"Do I have your word it won't leave this room?"

"No, you'll have to trust me."

"Okay. Earlier this year, I caught a big fish and a guy I know washed the money for me through a real estate deal."

"So, you're saying there's dirty money in Wharf Landing?"

Hans held out his palms, as if to push Jim away. "Whoa, I'm not saying that. All I know is I ended up there with a condo and a huge thirty-year mortgage."

"Look, Hans," I said. "I work for the medical examiner's office and we have a dead body without a name. This guy was shot in Wharf Landing on the night of August 22nd. You live in Wharf Landing. You know anything about that?"

His brows lifted. "Shot? I don't know anything about a murder. I'm a con artist, violence is above my paygrade."

"Sometimes even a good con goes bad," Jim said.

"Hey, check my rap sheet—nothing violent."

"Do you own a pistol?" I asked.

"A little 22 caliber peashooter."

"You sure it's not a 9mm?"

"Yeah, I'm sure."

"If violence is above your paygrade, why do you need a gun?"

"For protection. You see how I work. Every once in a

while, I get an angry client."

"Were you protecting yourself on the night of August 22nd?" Jim asked.

Sweat began to drip from Han's sideburns. "Hey, I've never shot anyone in my life." He raised his right hand. "I swear."

"Okay, we didn't say you shot him," Jim said. "But we need your help to find out who did."

Hans sat down on one of his card table chairs and dropped his head into his hands. "I, I can't."

"Why?" I asked.

"There are some high-powered people in my building, really bad asses. If they ever found out I ... oh, man, they'd cut my balls off."

"Tell you what," Jim said. "I'll give you twenty-four hours to think about it, but if you decide not to help us, ask your lawyer how many years you'll get for the tax evasion of about a million dollars. My guess is three to five. Oh, and you'll have to explain how you received the money in the first place. That should be worth another five or six."

"Okay, I get it. Give me your number. I'll call you tomorrow."

Jim handed Hans his card and poked his finger into his chest. "If you skip on me, I'm going to find those bad guys and I'm going to tell 'em you ratted 'em out."

"Don't do that, please. I won't skip."

~ * ~

On the way back to my office I asked Jim, "Why did you give him twenty-four hours?"

"I want to see what line of bullshit he comes up with."

"You don't really think he was involved, do you?"

"No, but I'm a cop, Rick. That's what we do."

CHAPTER TWENTY-ONE

I understand how hard it is for people from other countries to get jobs when they immigrate to the U.S. and that explains why so many are driving taxis. What I don't understand is why a driver would carry on a cell phone conversation with someone else, in a foreign language, while ignoring their source of income sitting in the back seat.

Today, when I got into a cab, the driver greeted me with a cell phone velcroed to his dash and a wire hanging from each ear. "Where to?" he asked.

"You know where the UCSF Medical Center is?"

"*Lo siento, pero no.* Yes, yes."

"You do or you don't?" I asked.

"Sorry, I was talking to someone else. Yes, I know this place."

I shrugged. "Okay, how about you take me there."

The ride from my office to the top of Parnassus Ave, where the medical center is located, took twenty-two minutes. The driver talked on his phone during twenty-one of them. I thought about stiffing him, but I knew he needed the money, so contrary to Stella's advice, I tipped him five bucks.

Dr. Eduardo Pérez shared a waiting room with

three other doctors in the Otolaryngology department. I phoned ahead and arranged for a ten-minute meeting, which was the maximum doled out to anyone not a patient. When I checked in at the reception desk, I was told the doctor would 'work me in' and I was asked to take a seat. I guess it was a busy day, I was 'worked in' an hour and forty minutes later.

An olive-skinned gentleman, about the same age as me, wearing a white coat and horn-rimmed glasses stood to greet me. "Dr. Rose ... Ed Pérez, nice to meet you. I understand you work for the ME."

"I'm her forensic odontologist, I work mainly on identifying John Does."

"So, Dr. Teeter said you stumbled on an adenoid cystic carcinoma of a sublingual salivary gland."

"Well, I didn't exactly stumble on it, I picked it up on an oral exam."

"That's fantastic. I didn't think corpses received that thorough an exam. So, what can I do for you?"

"You diagnosed an ACC about three months ago?"

"That's correct, I remember it because of how rare it is."

"Did you treat it?"

"No, I didn't."

"Why not?"

"The patient never returned."

"Any idea why?"

"Not really, I told him it could be terminal, but either he didn't believe me or he went elsewhere for treatment."

"Or didn't treat it at all."

"That would have been a poor choice, but I guess it's possible."

"Could you share his information with me?"

"Well, as you know, HIPAA laws prevent sharing without the patient's consent, however in this case I believe I can."

"Why's that?"

"I'm quite sure the patient gave us fraudulent information."

"How do you know it was fraudulent?"

"The man was Hispanic, but he registered as Joe Smith and when we sent him follow up information, the envelope came back as 'address unknown.'"

"So, when you say Hispanic, do you suspect he was from Mexico?"

"No, not at all. I'm from Mexico and I can easily recognize a Mexican accent. This man was from somewhere in South America—my guess Venezuela, Colombia, maybe even Peru."

"Would you be okay with giving me a copy of your findings?"

"Like I said, HIPAA doesn't apply here, so I'll have copies made for you before you leave."

I stood and offered him my hand. "Thanks, Dr. Pérez, you've been a great help."

"My pleasure." He glanced at his watch. "Whoops, I'm running late. Gotta run, good luck."

Just as I stepped out of the hospital building, a cab pulled to the curb and dropped off a guy and his two crutches. I peeked inside. "Can you take me downtown?"

The driver held a thumb in the air and with the other hand pulled down the handle on his meter. I slipped into the back seat and he took off. Unlike most of the other taxis I've taken in San Francisco, this one had a screen built into the back of the front seat and every thirty seconds a new advertisement popped up in front of me.

I did my best to ignore the screen but it was virtually impossible, so I watched. Most of the ads were for local businesses and events and were, to say the least, boring. Then one came on that piqued my interest. I grabbed a pen and on the back of one of my business cards I jotted a phone number. As soon as I got dropped off, I hustled up to my office and called it.

A woman sporting a Queen's English accent answered. "Welcome to Sotheby's International Realty. How may I direct your call?"

"I see from your ad there's a unit for sale at Wharf Landing. I'm interested in taking a look at it."

"Brilliant," she said. "May I have your name, sir?"

"Dr. Rose, Dr. Rick Rose."

"Thank you, Dr. Rose, if you will excuse a short hold, I'll put you through to Rebecca Halifax straight away."

Rebecca Halifax's accent wasn't Queen's English, but it was close. "Good afternoon, Dr. Rose, I hear you are interested in our Wharf Landing listing."

"I am. Is it still available?"

"It is, but I'm obligated to tell you the asking price before showing it to you. It's listed at 6.25 million. Would that be a barrier for you?"

"Not at all. Sounds like a pretty good price for Wharf Landing. When could I see it?"

"Anytime tomorrow afternoon would work. Shall I pick you up?"

I didn't want Rebecca Halifax to know I was a county employee. "No, I'll have my driver bring me. Two o'clock?"

"Wonderful," she said.

CHAPTER TWENTY-TWO

I set Stella's latte on her desk and stepped back waiting for her reaction. After running her tongue across the lid, she took a sip. "Oh, my God, that's good!"

"Like it?"

"Love it. What is it?"

"Josie's special of the week—banana caramel."

She took another gulp and closed her eyes. "No more talking right now, I'm in the middle of a foodgasm."

I'd never heard that word before, but it wasn't rocket science to figure out what it meant. We both sat back and silently finished our drinks. When I was sure there was nothing left in Stella's cup, I spoke. "Are you done with your 'gasm?"

"Totally. So, the secretary for some lawyer called. He said, Dr. Keller wanted him to speak with you."

"Did she leave a number?"

She handed me a Post-it. "Rick, are you in some kind of trouble?"

"Stella, you should know by now, I'm always in some kind of trouble."

"Can I help?"

"It's nothing to worry about." She gave me a questioning look. "Really," I said.

~ * ~

The lawyer Alex set me up with had a name that didn't fit his physical appearance. When I stepped into his office, he rose to greet me and held out his hand. He stood at least six foot seven and probably weighed two-sixty. "Teddy Small," he said. I had to hold back a grin.

"You can laugh, everyone does," he said. "You won't believe it, but that's also my dad's name, so technically I'm Teddy Small Jr."

I didn't laugh, but I did smile. "Rick Rose ... Dr. Keller sent me."

After a few more pleasantries, we sat at a conference table and Teddy set a yellow pad and a ballpoint pen in front of him. "Alex didn't tell me much, she said you would speak for yourself."

I nodded. "Sure. So, my job is to find the identities of John Does who come into our morgue. Right now, I'm working on a bizarre case where a guy without any ID jumped off the Golden Gate Bridge but ironically died of a gunshot wound inflicted earlier that evening."

"Okay, so far so good, you're not involved in a crime unless you shot the guy, which I doubt. Obviously, there's more."

"There is. The cab driver who drove him to the bridge wouldn't open up to the police, but he did to me, only after I promised to keep part of his story secret." I paused. "I assume telling you about it won't violate that promise."

"No worries, this conversation is protected by attorney-client privilege. I can't repeat it without your permission."

"That's what I thought. So, the cab driver told me that before the guy took the leap, he handed the driver a briefcase and told him it was for the driver's kids—for their education."

"He told you that."

"As I said, after I promised to keep it a secret."

Teddy's head was bobbing, ever so slightly, back and forth. "And the contents of the case is the secret you're talking about."

"Correct. It contained two hundred and fifty thousand in cash."

"And you're concerned the money may have been obtained illegally."

"Like during the commission of a crime, maybe. After all, the guy took a bullet to the chest. If I keep this to myself and then find out the money is tied to a crime, could the cabbie, his wife and I all be accessories after the fact?"

"Well, that depends."

"On what?"

"Not sure, depends on the crime. Have you told anyone other than me?"

"No one."

"How about Alex?"

"I told her I was worried about being an accessory to a crime, but I purposely didn't tell her about the briefcase or the money."

"Good." He paused. "I have the feeling there's more you want to tell me."

"Yeah, there is. I work closely with the homicide captain and one of his detectives and I lied to withhold this thing from them."

Teddy leaned back in his chair and like piecing together parts of a jigsaw puzzle, he let the synapses in his gray matter connect his thoughts. After five minutes of silence, he spoke. "So, let's not confuse a criminal dilemma with an ethical one. Right now, there is no evidence that the money is tied to a crime, so for now you don't have to be concerned with that. Your ethical predicament is different. You have an obligation to keep your police partners informed or at the least not mislead them, but you obtained this information by making a promise to the cab driver and his wife that you wouldn't do so; thus, creating an ethical dilemma."

"And, how do I resolve it?"

"You don't. By its very nature, it is unresolvable."

I knew I was caught in that tangled web of deceit without a way to free myself. "So, if I understand the upshot of our discussion, you suggest I do nothing?"

"For now ... yes. If the money gets tied to a crime, you and I will meet again to weigh your options. In the meantime, do what you're doing, but don't tell anyone about the money or your alliance with the cab driver."

I thanked Teddy Small and walked the mile and a half back to my office. I had to clear my head.

CHAPTER TWENTY-THREE

T he next day I made a point of getting to my office early. I knew Bruno worked graveyard, from midnight until about eight in the morning, so I figured if I called before nine, I could catch him before he hit the sack. I was right; his wife said he was just walking through the door and handed him the phone.

"Bruno, Dr. Rose here, any chance I could stop by for a short talk?"

"About what?"

"About our guy. I can be at your house in twenty minutes."

"I'm sorta beat, Doc. Had a drunk who wouldn't get outta the cab and it took two cops to drag the asshole out."

"I'll only take a half hour of your time. Promise."

There was a long pause. Then, "Okay, sure, see ya in twenty minutes."

~ * ~

When Bruno's wife opened the door, she gave me a suspicious look and didn't invite me inside. "You made us a promise," she said.

"And I intend to keep that promise, Mrs. Cappelletti. May I come in?"

That elicited at least a piece of a smile and the door

opened wider. As I entered, it crossed my mind that I may have just pounded another nail into my ethical coffin.

Bruno was sitting at the kitchen table eating what looked like a slice of a bacon and cheese frittata and drinking a cup of espresso. "Hey, Doc, can the Mrs. get you somethin' to eat?" He pointed to his plate. "Her special recipe—mozzarella, pancetta and basil."

"No thanks, just coffee sounds good."

"Italian or American?" Mrs. Cappelletti asked.

I pointed to the demitasse cup in front of Bruno. "Espresso's good … with two sugars, if you have them."

Bruno's wife set down a cup of dark, thick coffee along with a slice of lemon peel and two cubes of brown sugar. "May I stay?" she asked.

"Certainly," I said. I looked at Bruno. "So, tell me again what you remember about the jumper."

He pointed to his cup and his wife refilled it. "What d'ya mean?" he asked.

"You said you didn't know he'd been shot, but you said he didn't look well."

"Yeah, that's right, he was pale and sweaty and talked kinda jerky."

"Jerky?"

"You know, start, stop, start again. That kinda jerky. But he seemed like a good guy. Asked me about my kids. Even after he pointed the gun at me and told me to stop the car he said please."

"Did he have an accent when he spoke?"

Bruno grew pensive, challenging his mind to recreate his conversation with the jumper. "Yeah, now that I think about it, he sounded a lot like Manny Garcia."

"Who's Manny Garcia?"

"Another cab driver I know, a Mexican guy. Actually,

he was born here, but his parents came from Mexico. He kinda talks English with a little Spanish sound."

"So, you think our guy may have been from south of the border somewhere?"

"I don't know geography very good, but I guess so … maybe."

"That's great information, Bruno. So, other than you, who else saw this guy when he got into your cab?"

He scratched his head for a moment. "Well, the door-man for sure."

"Anyone else?"

"There coulda been somebody inside the doors."

"Inside? How could you see someone inside?"

"When the guy came through the doors with the briefcase, he looked back and I thought I saw like a shadow or somethin'. Then the doors closed behind him and he hurried to my cab."

Bruno's last statement lit a bulb in my brain. "The briefcase, what did it look like?"

"I dunno, a briefcase."

"Cloth, leather?"

"Leather."

"Black, brown?"

"Hey, forget all these questions, ya wanna see it?"

If Bruno had hit me over the head with a baseball bat, I wouldn't have been more startled. "You still have it?" I blurted.

"Yeah, why throw out a good piece of leather?" He nodded to his wife and she scurried out of the room. In less than a minute she returned holding a black leather briefcase and handed it to me.

In all the TV mysteries, when the detective looks inside the missing case he finds a clue, like a card, a receipt or a scrap of paper with a note on it. I was not that lucky; this case was totally empty. "Can I take it with me?" I asked.

"Remember your promise," Mrs. Cappelletti said.

"Don't worry, no one will ever know what was in it."

~ * ~

After getting back to my office I spent an hour examining the briefcase. This wasn't a cheap knockoff from China, it was a piece of art. The leather was of the highest quality—soft and smooth. The stitching was clean and precise. A beautiful butterfly logo was printed on the outside and inside was sewed the company label written in Classic Copperplate script. It read: *Mario Fernández – Bogotá, CO, 23-106*

Neiman Marcus was less than a mile's walk away. I placed the case in a shopping bag and headed over there. The leather department carried five brands of briefcases. The cheapest, a Ferragamo, was on sale for $1995. The most expensive, a Bottega Veneta, was priced at $9200.

I opened my shopping bag and handed the manager the case Bruno had given me. "Ever hear of this brand?"

He turned it over as he massaged the leather, then he inspected the inside and checked the label. "This is a very high-quality bag. We've never carried this brand, but I'd say it's certainly in the Bottega Veneta class."

"So, it sold for somewhere around ten grand."

"That's my opinion, yes."

"Other than Neiman, who in San Francisco might carry a case of this quality?"

The manager bit his lip as he thought about the question. "Probably, only one shop, Jean Pierre Leather on Maiden Lane."

Maiden Lane, one of the city's oldest streets, is a pedestrian mall not far from Union Square. If you're looking for a bargain you don't shop for anything on this street. I stepped into Jean Pierre's and was greeted by a gray-haired man in his sixties, wearing a three-piece suit and a pair of shoes so highly polished, I could almost see my reflection in them. I handed him the briefcase. "The manager at Neiman's thought you might carry this brand."

He went through the same drill—massaging and inspecting. "I don't carry it," he said. "As you can see, this company is in Bogotá, Colombia. I've heard of it, but I've never seen one of their bags until now. If I remember correctly, they don't sell to the U.S. market." He held up a finger. "Hold on, I'll be right back."

In a minute or two he returned, clutching a catalogue the size of the Old Testament. He flipped through the pages until he reached the M's. "Here it is, Mario Fernández. I was right, they don't sell in the U.S."

"So where do think it was bought?"

"Looks like they're only sold where they're manufactured."

"I thought Colombia's a poor country, how can anyone there afford them?"

The man laughed. "Believe me, sir, there are rich people everywhere in the world."

CHAPTER TWENTY-FOUR

M y upcoming meeting with Rebecca Halifax would not be without pitfalls. If I wanted to keep up my charade as a wealthy doctor, I'd have to show up in a fancy car, preferably driven by a chauffeur. If I accidentally ran into Adriana Vargas, the managing director of Wharf Landing, she'd know I wasn't there to look at real estate and would no doubt expose me. The first problem I could handle, the second was totally up to fate.

I phoned my neighbor, Jacques Devereaux. "*Bonjour, Docteur* Rick," he answered. "How is the new romance going?"

"I wouldn't call it a romance, just a nice relationship."

"That is not what I hear, *mon cher ami*."

Even though Jacques had introduced me to Frankie, I didn't feel comfortable discussing our relationship with him. "Ever hear that curiosity killed the cat?"

"Cat? Your cat died?"

"No, never mind, I need a favor."

"Of course, fire the gun."

"You mean, shoot."

"*Pardon.*"

"In America, when you want someone to speak up, you say 'shoot' not fire the gun."

"Okay then, shoot."

"Do you still have that monster Mercedes you bought last year?"

"It's a 4-door S-Class, not a monster, and yes, I still have it."

"Would you drive me to an appointment this afternoon?"

"No, but I'll loan you ten dollars for a cab."

"I need to arrive in a fancy car."

"You mean in a monster?"

"Okay, sorry about that, will you drive me?"

"Will it be worth another dinner at Frascati?"

I sighed. "Yes … it will. Pick me up at two."

I would have liked to have shown up in a suit and tie, but as I said earlier, the only suit I had was a leftover from my wedding ten years ago. If it still fit, which was unlikely, it would no doubt be out of style. I decided to wear the new sport coat and slacks I'd bought for my date with Frankie.

Jacques honked the horn at ten minutes after two. I gave Einstein a Blue Buffalo Burst Cat Treat and headed for the back seat of the Mercedes S-Class. "Hey, you're supposed to open the back door for me," I said.

"Who says?"

"I need it to look like this is a limo."

"Fine, I'll do it when we get there. Give me the address for the GPS."

Jacques input the numbers for Wharf Landing and we took off. "What time is your appointment?" he asked.

"Two o'clock."

He looked at his watch. "It's already twenty after."

"No problem, rich people move to their own schedules."

Jacques kept his word. After pulling up in front of the building where Rebecca Halifax was waiting, he jumped out of the driver's seat and opened the Mercedes' back door. Before stepping out, I said, "Go ahead of me and check the managing director's office. If she's in there, keep her there until we're on the elevator."

"How do I do that?"

"I don't know, you're the psychiatrist, you'll figure it out."

Ms. Halifax, an exceedingly attractive and well-dressed woman in her middle thirties, spotted me as soon as I stepped out of the Mercedes. "Dr. Rose, welcome ... call me Rebecca. Did you hit traffic coming over?"

"Not really. Why, am I late?"

"No, no, right on time. What's with your driver, though, he almost knocked me over to get inside the building."

"Yes, sorry about that. Plumbing problem ... he has to pee every twenty minutes. So, on which floor is the unit you're showing me?"

"Second, the least expensive floor. Shall we explore?"

The doorman, the same one Jim and I questioned a couple days earlier, let us into the rotunda. If he recognized me, he didn't show it. I did a quick 360° scan for any sign of Adriana Vargas, but neither she nor Jacques was anywhere to be seen. Rebecca Halifax and I got into the elevator.

When the doors slid open, we stepped onto a red plush pile carpet that lined the hallway. "There are five units on each of the floors," Rebecca said. "This one has a wonderful northern exposure." We stepped into a room featuring an all-glass wall with views of the bay, both bridges, Alcatraz and Marin County. "This apartment is

3240 square feet, with this great room accounting for 1800 of it. The 20-foot ceilings make it look quite a bit larger, don't you think?" I nodded and couldn't help but wonder who did the dusting.

She led me into the kitchen which was lined with wall-to-wall stainless-steel appliances—everything from a walk-in refrigerator/freezer to a specialty-drink coffee maker. "You're the first to inquire about this condo. Where did you see the ad?" she asked.

"In the backseat of a cab."

"We only placed that ad a couple of days ago; I guess they work. So, shall we look at the bedrooms and the den?"

The bedrooms also had high ceilings along with adjoining baths. The master featured two showers, four sinks, a Jacuzzi and a hot tub. From the master, we walked into the den. It was a man-cave. There was a teakwood desk, four matching chairs, a couch, one full wall dedicated to video games, and another that featured an 84 inch Samsung TV. I walked around the desk and, knowing this was a snooping mission, turned over an envelope that was lying on top of it. It was addressed to none other than Hans Van den Brink.

"When is this owner moving out?" I asked.

"Oh, he's already gone. Business out of the country, I believe."

"Huh, what if I were to give you a check for 6.25 million today, how would you get ahold of him?"

"Nowadays all the papers can be signed electronically, but his lawyer would handle the escrow to pay off the loan."

"So, there's a mortgage on it?"

"Oh, yes, a large one I believe, but no worries, his lawyer will clear the title for you."

We took the elevator back to the rotunda and I held my hand out signaling Rebecca to step out first. It wasn't about being polite, I was looking out for Adriana Vargas. Other than the doorman, the rotunda was empty.

"May I call you after you've had some time to think about it?" Rebecca asked.

"Of course, you have my number."

We shook hands and went to our respective vehicles, my Mercedes and her Jaguar. As I approached mine, Jacques popped out of the front seat and opened the back door. "Did you find the managing director?" I asked.

"I did. She's an unbelievably beautiful woman. We're going to dinner tomorrow night."

"Wow, you French guys live up to your reputation. Just don't spill the beans."

"I'm not ordering beans."

"I know. It's a saying that means, don't reveal today's subterfuge."

"Ah, don't worry, we French are quite discreet."

Jacques headed the S-Class monster in the direction of home and I dialed Jim. "That you, Rick," he answered.

"Yeah, we have a problem."

"What?"

"Hans skipped."

CHAPTER TWENTY-FIVE

I knew that night I'd have to make another trip back to Wharf Landing. The daytime doorman told us that the guy on duty during the evening of August 21st and the early hours of August 22nd was a guy named Sam Woodruff. Other than Bruno, he was the last person to see the jumper alive.

I didn't want to interrupt him during his busy hours, so I set my alarm for 1:00 a.m. and caught a cat nap for three hours. That was just long enough to have another one of my crazy dreams.

I was lounging around in the northern exposure condo at Wharf Landing. Suddenly, there was a loud knock on the door. I looked at my watch, it was three in the morning. I knew I shouldn't answer the door, but I did. A man whose face I couldn't make out stood before me, holding a gun in his right hand and a black briefcase in his left. I don't know why, but I pulled the case from his hand and raced to the outside deck. I heard a shot and felt a burning in my back. I was trapped with nowhere to go. I looked over the railing. I jumped. Like my last dream, I woke up drenched in sweat.

I called for a cab, which arrived a little before two and dropped me off at Wharf Landing at two-twenty. The fog had come in and so had a brisk breeze; the doorman was parked inside, rubbing his hands together to stay warm. When he saw me approach, he stepped out. "Help you, sir?"

"Yeah, are you Sam Woodruff?"

He didn't appear at all surprised that I knew his name. "Yes, sir."

"Detective Allen and I talked to your daytime guy about a week ago. Maybe he mentioned it to you."

"He did. I figured you'd be here one of these nights."

"So, do you remember a man leaving the building between 3:00 and 3:30 on Friday August 22nd?"

"No, not offhand."

"Really? How many people usually come in and out of here at that hour?"

"I don't know, not many."

"You opened the door for this guy. He was carrying a black briefcase." I pointed toward the curb. "He got into a cab, right over there."

"If you say so, sir."

"It's not important what I say, do you remember the guy or not?"

"No."

"The guy was injured. He had trouble walking."

"I didn't see him, sir."

"The guy had been shot. He died a half hour after you saw him."

"I didn't see him."

"The cab driver said you did."

"Well, he's mistaken."

"Do you know the guy who lives in the northern exposure unit on the 2nd floor?"

"Sir, I open doors for the owners, I don't hang around

with 'em."

"Do any of the owners ever tip you?"

"Some, once in a while."

"Who tipped you to shut up about August 22nd?"

"No one."

"Any idea how long you could go to jail for lying about this?"

"No, sir, I'm not a lawyer."

"Well, you may be needing one soon." I handed him my card. "If your memory gets better, give me a call. Otherwise, expect a visit from a homicide detective."

~ * ~

I don't do well when I'm short on sleep and it was close to four by the time I flopped into bed. Stella would have to do without her morning latte, I didn't stumble into the office until noon.

"You look awful," Stella said. "Late night?"

"Yeah, but not what you're thinking."

"How do you know what I'm thinking?"

"I just do. So, any calls?"

"Detective Allen called four times. I don't know what you said to him, but instead of asking about my bra size or my libido, he asked how my day was going."

"That's good. What else did he say?"

"He said he'd be in his office all day and he needs to talk to you."

I knew, when I made the promise to Bruno and his wife, I would be compromising my relationship with the SFPD—namely homicide detective Jim Allen and homicide captain Mike Kelly—but I didn't calculate how badly. The jumper carried a briefcase containing a quarter million in cash and before he took the leap, he gave the case and the money to his cab driver. I knew that the case came from Colombia and maybe our John Doe did too. My job is only to ID a corpse, theirs is to solve a murder. How long, in good conscience, could I withhold information from them?

When I stepped into Jim's cubicle, Mike Kelly was there also. "We were just talking about you," Mike said.

"Really. Why?"

"I was thinking I may hire you away from Alex and put you on my detective payroll."

"That would be the day. I'm still trying to justify my job as a forensic odontologist."

"Jim brought me up to speed on this Hans guy. You think he may be the one who shot the jumper?"

"I doubt it. What're the odds that the guy who conned my ex-wife out of a few bucks is the same guy behind the murder of our John Doe?"

"A million to one, I get it. But if he's not our guy, why did he disappear after you and Jim interviewed him?"

"Maybe he knows who did do it and he's scared shitless. Look, the jumper was shot in Wharf Landing; I doubt by Hans Van den Brink, but still in Wharf Landing. My guess is by one of the other condominium owners. Whoever that is, got to the doorman. He denies ever seeing our guy, even though the cab driver swears he opened the door for the man. Maybe you guys should lean on him."

Mike looked at Jim. "How about you get on that." He turned to me. "I hear you got the information about Wharf Landing from the cab driver. Did he give you anything else we can use?"

My dilemma raised its ugly head again. Tell the truth and betray my promise to the Cappellettis or lie and betray the people who I work with and who trust me. Maybe revealing part of the truth would be better than lying about all of it. "He gave me a briefcase that the jumper left behind in the cab."

"Really. What was in it?"

Damn it, I was right back where I started a minute ago. "Nothing, he said it was empty."

"So, it doesn't tell us anything?"

Be careful, but be truthful, I told myself, as truthful as you can. "I checked it out. It was bought in Bogotá, Columbia."

"So, you think our guy was from South America?"

"Yeah, I do. The jumper had a malignant tumor growing under his tongue and I checked out some cancer treatment centers in the city. A doctor who examined him pegged his accent as maybe Venezuelan, Colombian or Peruvian."

Mike leaned back and processed the information. "A lot of drugs come out of Colombia, maybe this was a drug deal gone bad. Rick, while Jim leans on the doorman, how about you go over that list of owners again, maybe something will ring a bell."

CHAPTER TWENTY-SIX

I scanned the Wharf Landing owner list and it took less than two minutes to pick out a common denominator. All the units on the 5th and 6th floors were owned by people with names ending with a Z: López, Martínez, Álvarez, Hernández, Suárez, Ramírez, Muñoz, Núñez. What did I conclude from this? Only that there are many Hispanic multi-millionaires living in San Francisco and several of them live on the top floors of Wharf Landing. I decided to drop in on Adriana Vargas.

Her secretary showed me in and I took a seat facing her desk. Jacques was right when he said Adriana Vargas is an unbelievably beautiful woman. Although I'm horrible at determining a woman's age, my uneducated guess would be early fifties, though she could easily pass for forty. Her black hair was tied in a tight, slicked back style that shimmered in contrast to her blue eyes. Her figure was perfect and she wore an outfit that put it readily on display.

"Dr. Rose, I sent Detective Allen the list of owners, what more do you need?" she asked.

"Just a little clarification."

"Clarification? It's a list, what is there to clarify?"

"I found it strange that so many of the owners on the

top floors are Hispanic. How do you account for that?"

"And what prejudices do you harbor against Hispanic people, Dr. Rose?"

"None. I'm just curious about the demographic in Wharf Landing."

"You may not have noticed, but there is a xenophobic stench polluting the air of this country. Hispanic people feel more comfortable around their own. I'm sure even you can understand that."

"I do understand, Ms. Vargas. I'm just curious if those owners hail from the same country."

"And why would that information be any of your business?"

"I believe the man who was shot in this building may have come from South America. Are any of your owners from South America?"

She tapped a cigarette from an open pack, placed it between her lips and lit it. After a deep inhale, she expelled the smoke, like a flame thrower, in my direction. "You, arrogant, bigoted, son of a bitch. You think you can come in here, throw your title around and expect me to kowtow to you? Fuck you, Dr. Rose, get the hell out of my office. And if you want any more personal information on my tenants, you can talk to my lawyer." She pushed her chair back and walked out of the office, leaving me alone with my ego in shreds and my tail between my legs.

~ * ~

When I walked into my office, Stella took one look and said, "Rick, what's wrong?"

"What? Nothing."

"Really? You have the same look you had when your last girlfriend sent you that 'Dear John' letter. Don't tell me your new *femme* ..."

"No, she's great, but I just got my metaphorical ass kicked by another woman."

"You're dating two women?"

"No, today's wasn't a date, it was an interrogation. I went to see the woman who manages Wharf Landing."

"You interrogated her?"

"It started out that way, but she managed to make it all about me. Now I feel like a jerk."

"Were you?"

"Was I what?"

"A jerk."

I pretended to ponder the question, but I already knew the answer. "Yeah, I was."

"Did you apologize?"

"I didn't have a chance, she walked out on me."

"So, does it really matter? You'll probably never see her again."

"Oh, I have the feeling I'll see her again. Just not sure when or why."

"Rick, if you're going to take on the job of a detective, you're going to have to grow a thicker skin or it will tear you apart."

I knew she was right. I'd been through situations like this before and, like this one, I let them get to my core. "I'll try," I said.

"You need a vacation from this case."

I shook my head. "Uh-uh, I'm going to find out who this poor guy was and when I do, I'll know who shot him and why he did a two and a half gainer off the bridge."

Then Stella did the darndest thing. She put her arms around my waist and rested her head on my chest. "You're a good guy, Rick. Someday I'm going to find a man like you."

I was touched by her admiration, but I didn't deserve it. She was picturing me as a knight on a white horse; I felt more like a pretender riding an old nag. "You can do better," I said.

She stepped back. There were tears in her eyes. "Damn it, Rick, why can't you see in yourself what everyone else sees in you?"

When I don't have an answer to a reasonable question, I usually make a joke, but I didn't want to trivialize her feelings with levity. "Thanks, Stella," I said. "You'll find that guy one day."

~ * ~

I spent the rest of the afternoon at my desk thinking about what Stella said. I'd had several successes working for the medical examiner, but I could never seem to balance them against my failures: my broken marriage, my addiction to alcohol, the loss of my dental practice. Maybe it was time to try harder. And maybe Stella was right about a vacation. It didn't need to be two weeks; it could be two days.

I tapped my speed dial. "*Allô*, Rick," she answered.

"Hey, Frankie, remember I promised to take you up to Mendocino for a couple days?"

"Men ... do ... cino, yes, I remember."

"You free this weekend?"

"If I wasn't I'd lie. Are we going on a trip?"

"Just pack jeans, tee shirts and a warm jacket. I'll pick you up tomorrow at three."

"I'll be ready."

"That's great. Oh ... uh ... the room at my favorite bed and breakfast only has a queen bed. Should I look for a place with twins?"

"Do you snore?"

"I don't think so."
"Neither do I, the queen bed will be fine."

CHAPTER TWENTY-SEVEN

T he next day was a short one for me. It was Friday and I was taking my first weekend vacation in four years. I figured if I worked till noon, I'd have enough time to pick up my car at Hertz, pack a few clothes, settle Einstein in with Josie, and get to Frankie's apartment by 3:00.

I gave Jim a call. He answered, as he often does, with an attitude. "Detective Allen, I'm in a hurry."

"Jim, it's me, Rick."

"Oh, sorry, I didn't check the ID. What's up?"

"Did you get a chance to talk to that night doorman?"

"Yeah, last night. He's sticking to his story about not seeing the jumper come outta the building that night."

"Did you squeeze him?"

"The usual, two years for lying to a police officer, three years for concealing evidence, five for accepting a bribe and twenty for being an accessory to murder."

"No reaction at all?"

"Didn't even flinch."

"That's not good."

"Don't worry, we'll get another shot at him."

"Any idea where Hans disappeared to?"

"I'm having my people check all the cabs and airlines,

we'll find him. I'll let you know. What time do you leave the office?"

"Today, I'm leaving at noon. Going out of town for the weekend."

A muffled chuckle came through the phone, followed by a sing-song voice. "Ricky has a girlfriend … Ricky has a girlfriend."

"She's a woman and she's just a friend. Okay?"

"Whatever you say, Ricky."

I decided, next time I'd tell Jim I was leaving work with the flu. "Talk to you Monday." I hung up.

~ * ~

My first stop was the Hertz agency on Twelfth and Folsom Streets. I'd reserved a Chevy Malibu, but as I stepped into the office a guy dropped off a candy-apple-red Corvette. "What's that one go for?" I asked.

The guy behind the counter stretched his neck to peek through the window. "Oh, the manager drives that one."

"So, Hertz owns it and the manager hogs it?"

"Well, you could put it that way."

"Tell him I want it for the weekend. He can drive my Malibu."

"Yeah … I don't think he'll go for that."

I handed him a couple of ten-dollar bills. "Tell him my uncle works at the head office in Estero Florida. He's in charge of customer complaints."

A few minutes later, the manager, with a scowl wrapped across his face, came into the office and handed me the keys. "Enjoy," he said, and stomped out.

~ * ~

They say cats have nine lives, well I swear they also have a sixth sense. Even before I took my overnight case

137

from the closet, Einstein bolted out of the room and disappeared. It took me forty-five minutes to find him; he was behind the clothes dryer. When I reached in to grab him, he put his claws out and tore five perfect lines of blood across the back of my hand. "Goddammit, Einstein, come out or you stay home alone for the weekend."

He wouldn't budge, so I left him there while I went into the bathroom to stop the bleeding. When I came back, he was still cemented in the same spot. I looked at my watch, it was a little after two and I still had to drop him off at Josie's before I picked up Frankie. "Okay, buddy, here comes the broom." I jammed the handle into the spot where the assault on my hand took place and poked it a couple times. White fur slowly appeared as Einstein slithered out of his hiding spot. He tried to run, but I grabbed him and tossed him into his crate.

When I dropped him off at Josie's apartment, she looked at the blood-soaked gauze around my hand. "Gotcha again, huh?"

"Little prick. You can keep him, I've had it."

Josie lifted him out of the crate and he was the perfect gentleman—nuzzling, purring and licking the back of her hand. "It must be you, he's just so sweet," she said.

"He's schizo. Give him a little time, he'll get you too." I set down six cans of salmon pâté and headed out.

~ * ~

Frankie had invited me up to her apartment after our first date, but I declined. This would be my first visit. I tapped lightly on the door and it opened before I could pull my hand away. "*Allô*, Rick, come in," she said. "I'm just about finished packing."

As I mentioned earlier, Nob Hill is a fancy address in San Francisco. Most of the apartment buildings were built after the 1906 fire on prime real estate. The granite plaque on the outside of this one read 1926.

The living room where I was waiting was huge. The ceiling reached at least twenty feet and four large windows offered an unobstructed view of the bay. With its lacquered mahogany and luxurious fabrics, the furniture was from another era.

"You like it?"

I turned to see Frankie wheeling a Louis Vuitton carry-on into the room. "The apartment? I love it. I may be wrong but this furniture looks antique French."

"It is. Almost a hundred years old." She couldn't miss my puzzled look. "This apartment, and everything in it, has been owned by family since 1928," she said.

"That's incredible. So, your family visits the U.S. quite often?"

"They used to. I'll tell you about it at dinner."

I grabbed Frankie's case and we headed for the car. When I popped the trunk on the Corvette, she said, "It looks like I'm not the only one with family secrets."

"I wish. Unfortunately, this is a rental." I checked the time. "The Pacific Coast highway is beautiful, but it's curvy and slow. We'll take it on the way back, but the 101 will get us up there in time for a late dinner."

~ * ~

The Albion River Inn is built on a high cliff overlooking the mouth of the river where it spills into the Pacific Ocean. I booked the cottage on the point and we pulled into its parking lot a little after seven. Following an awkward discussion of bathroom privacy, we took turns showering and then strolled to the restaurant.

"So, this is where that Petrale fish is caught?" Frankie asked.

"Well, a few miles offshore but, yes, this is where it happens."

The maître d' seated us next to a window just in time to witness the sun transform into a distorted orange ball and dissolve below the horizon. Frankie put her hand on top of mine. "This is beautiful, Rick, thanks for bringing me here."

I smiled, like a weekend date was something I do all the time, but it wasn't. I really liked Frankie and I think she liked me, but I knew nothing could screw up a relationship faster than a guy looking for sex on their first overnight. So, I decided if it were to happen, she would have to be the one to initiate it. "You're welcome," I said. "I've been looking forward to this weekend too." I glanced at the menu. "So, looks like we're ordering Petrale again."

Being a recovering alcoholic can really suck. Frankie ordered a nice Grgich Hills Chardonnay with her meal while I was stuck with a cheap zero-proof wine that tasted more like grape juice mixed with vinegar. "So, what's with the apartment on Nob Hill?" I asked.

"It's one of many. My family owns properties around the world, but my father is not well, so they don't travel any longer."

"Nothing serious, I hope."

"Congestive heart failure, so it's not good. He retired last year."

"Sorry to hear that. What type of work did he do?"

"A banker."

"Oh, which bank?"

"Have you heard of the Banque de France?"

"Thee … Banque de France?"

"Yes, that one. My father's, great, great … great, great, grandfather founded it in 1850."

I tried to act as if dating a woman who was exceedingly wealthy didn't faze me, but it did. I began to question if Francoise Barbier was out of my league. It must have shown. "Will this be a problem to our relationship?" she asked.

I recovered from the shock and this time put my hand on hers. "As long as we don't have a 'meet the parent's moment', it won't."

"I would never spring that upon you, I promise. Let's just enjoy this time together. Yes?"

And that's exactly what we did.

~ * ~

For the trip back to San Francisco, as I promised, we drove the Pacific Coast Highway with its curves, cliffs and spectacular views. It took almost six hours but it was worth it. We pulled up in front of Frankie's apartment building a little after 9:00 p.m.

"I had a wonderful time," she said.

"So did I."

"Can we do it again sometime?"

"Of course, why would we not?" I asked.

She gave me a sly smile. "I don't know. I felt I may have been a little ... how do you say it in English? Over aggressive."

I pulled her close to me and gave her a kiss. "No, you were perfect."

CHAPTER TWENTY-EIGHT

T he first thing I did Monday morning was to call Jacques Devereaux. I owed him a dinner for acting as my chauffeur the day I met the realtor at Wharf Landing, but that wasn't the reason I wanted to pay my debt. Jacques managed a date with Adriana Vargas and knowing him, the quintessential psychiatrist, he now possessed a wealth of information about her personal life.

He answered in his usual annoying way. *"Bonjour, mon ami."*

"Hi, Jacques. I owe you one at Frascati's."

"You're actually going to make good on that?"

"Of course. How about tonight, seven o'clock?"

"Make it six forty-five."

"Fine, see you there."

I decided it was high time I brought my boss back into this case. Her secretary told me to go right in. As usual, I tapped twice, opened the door and stepped in. She looked up, "Rick, I guess the rumor was correct."

"What rumor is that?"

"That you still work for the medical examiner."

I'd never witnessed Alex give someone a dressing down, but I was pretty sure I was now. "I apologize," I said. "I've been really wrapped up in this jumper thing. If I bring you up to speed, will you forgive me?"

She smiled, like she always did. "I'm not mad, Rick, I just like to be kept in the loop."

"I know you do … again, sorry."

"Forgiven. Now, have a seat and let's hear where you are in this case."

I pulled up a chair across from her desk. "Some of this you know, but I'll start from the beginning anyhow. Our John Doe came out of Wharf Landing and got into Bruno Cappelletti's cab at three in the morning and we know Bruno drove him to the middle of the Golden Gate Bridge. He ordered Bruno to stop at the mid-span, then he limped out of the cab. But, before he did, he gave Bruno a briefcase filled with …" I almost slipped but caught myself.

"Filled with what?" Alex asked.

"I can't tell you, at least not now."

"It's that thing you talked to the lawyer about, isn't it?"

"Yeah. Right now, I'm the only one at risk. If I tell you, then you're in the boiling water with me."

"I get it. Okay, what next?"

"I had an expert at Jean Pierre's Leather Shop examine the case and he was almost certain it was bought in Colombia."

"Colombia? Do you think our guy was from Colombia?"

"Maybe. So, there's no doubt that John Doe jumped off the bridge, but his suicide attempt failed. As you know, Helmut determined the man died of a gunshot wound, most likely inflicted at Wharf Landing, before he hit the water."

"Right, I knew that."

"So, you were with me on the exam of the victim's mouth, when we discovered the tumor that had been growing under his tongue. Helmut later confirmed it was an adenoid cystic carcinoma, a very rare, very aggressive cancer. I know our guy was aware that the tumor was likely terminal because when I interviewed Dr. Eduardo Pérez, the ENT doc who examined him, he told me he'd informed the patient of that risk."

"I assume he didn't get it treated?"

"Doesn't look like it. Dr. Pérez gave me another important piece of information, though. He said the patient went by the name of Joe Smith but he was Hispanic and spoke English with what sounded like a South American accent—maybe Venezuelan, Peruvian or Colombian"

"So, the jumper is probably from Colombia."

"I said, maybe."

"What do you and Jim know about Wharf Landing? Sounds like that's where this case gets solved."

"Another maybe. The director of Wharf Landing is a woman named Adriana Vargas and she's not what I would describe as forthcoming. Jim had to coerce the Wharf Landing owner's list out of her by threatening a total building search by the police."

"And?"

"All of the top floor units are owned by people with South American names, again maybe Colombian. I went back and interviewed her about it, but she threw the xenophobic, race card at me."

"I apologize, Rick."

"Apologize? For what?"

"For thinking you were sitting on your butt."

"Well, I still should have kept you in the loop. Look, I've been thinking about something. We're pretty sure the jumper was shot in Wharf Landing, which means in one of those twenty-four units and we've been going on the theory that he was a visitor there. But what if he wasn't? What if he lived there?"

Alex had a twisted grin. "Then his name is on the list."

"Exactly. Adriana Vargas knows more than she's telling us, which isn't much. I'll know a little more about her tonight."

Alex' eyebrows lifted. "You don't have a date with her, do you?"

"No, it's better than that. I have a date with the guy who had a date with her."

~ * ~

I got to Frascati at exactly 6:45 and was greeted by Matteo, the maître d'. *"Buonasera, Dottore Rose.* Just you tonight?"

"No, the French guy who doesn't like Italian food is joining me."

"Oh, yes, the head doctor. I'll seat you now and send him back when he arrives."

Quite a while later I saw Matteo leading Jacques to the table. I glanced at my watch, it was after 7:15. As soon as he was seated, I said, "Why did you say seven was too early?"

"I never said that."

"Yes, you did."

"I said, 'make it six-forty-five.'"

"Why did you do that? It's after seven."

"Control, *mon ami.* We psychiatrists like control."

"Great, how about you take control of the check tonight?"

Jacques broke up laughing. "Ah, you're such a kidder,

are you not?"

I caved. "Yeah, just kidding." I picked up the menu. "Hey, they have a French dish, *ris d'agneau.*"

"Ugh, that's sweetbreads, I don't eat glandular meat. I'll acquiesce and get the Bucatini with sausage and peppers."

We made small talk until the dessert arrived. "So, how was your date with the dragon lady?" I asked.

"Dragon lady? What is that … dragon lady?"

"Never mind. How was your date with Adriana Vargas?"

"Ah, wonderful, such a beautiful woman."

"I don't think she likes me."

"You are very perceptive, Rick, she loathes you. She called you a racist porker."

"I think you mean pig."

"That's it, a racist pig."

"Why, just because I wanted to know the demographic of some of the Wharf Landing owners?"

"I believe that was the reason, yes."

"All I asked was if any of her occupants came from South America. Is that racist?"

"I don't know, you tell me."

"Look, Jacques, I'm not one of your patients, so don't make me answer my own questions. She's from South America and I touched a nerve. Right?"

"Perhaps."

"I'm wondering, is she from Colombia?"

"I have no idea."

"I thought she might be, but her name doesn't sound Colombian."

"Why do you say that?"

"I looked it up, most Colombian names end with a Z."

"I believe your information is fallacious."

"So, you think she could be Colombian."

"She could."

"Any idea how she got the job at Wharf Landing?"

"She said through a friend."

"Does her friend live there?"

"She didn't say."

"She dresses wealthy. Is she?"

"I didn't ask for her financial statement."

"Where did you take her?"

"A place called Gary Danko."

I knew the Gary Danko restaurant very well. I met with a guy there once, who turned out to be a spy, and I walked out on a three-hundred-dollar meal. "Wow, I didn't think you would spring that much for a dinner."

"Adriana chose it and I didn't want to disappoint. Hey, enough already, just stop, okay?"

"Stop what?"

"The cross examination. I feel like I'm on trial."

"Oh, sorry, I'm just interested in your social life, that's all."

"I'm a psychiatrist, remember? You're not interested in me at all. You're interested in Adriana Vargas and I've told you all I know. So, pay the check and let's get out of here."

CHAPTER TWENTY-NINE

One of the advantages of getting to work late is the absence of a line in front of Josie's Java truck. I stepped right up to the window. "Making Stella wait for her morning latte?" Josie asked.

"Looks that way. Hey, you spoiled our furry friend. He jumped on and off my bed all night. What did you let him get away with anyway?"

"I let him sleep under the covers. Try it, he dozed right off."

"Cat's sleep ninety percent of their lives away. I don't want to add to the last ten percent."

"Suit yourself." She handed me the coffees and as usual I handed her a twenty.

~ * ~

"Are you okay?" Stella asked as she popped the top off one of the paper cups.

"Yeah, why?"

"You're only late when you've had a bad night."

I didn't want to waste her time complaining about a schizophrenic cat, so I lied. "Nope, slept fine, just took an extra hour of personal time. After you finish your coffee, give Jim Allen a buzz for me. Tell him I'm coming over to the station in half an hour."

~ * ~

With files strewn all over the floor, Jim's cubicle was a mess. "I didn't think you were working these many cases at once," I said.

He laughed. "I'm not, but it looks that way, doesn't it?"

"Well, I hope the jumper's file is somewhere in that mess."

He tapped a manilla folder laying on top of his desk. "Right here. Wanna know where Hans Van den Brink took off to?"

"That's why I'm here."

"Santa Fe."

"Santa Fe? How do you know?"

"We tracked down an Uber that dropped him at the airport at 2:38 a.m. Only sixteen domestic flights took off between three and four, so I checked the security cameras for all of them. He boarded a Southwest flight that left at 3:52."

"So, he's in Santa Fe, but who knows where in Santa Fe?"

"34725 Dusty Ranch Road."

"How ..."

"This guy loves booking Ubers."

Jim could be a real asshole at times, but that didn't detract from his detective skills. I figured he had more to tell me. "You wouldn't happen to know who owns the house at 34725 Dusty Ranch Road, would you?"

He grinned. "A divorcee named Mildred Lamson."

"So, he's shacking up."

"Looks that way. Should I have the local cops pick him up?"

I thought about the question. Hans is a jerk, but he

didn't strike me as a murderer and I didn't know what we'd do with him once we brought him back. Jim could charge him for swindling Josie, but that would only be a distraction right now. "Any way, we can just keep an eye on him?" I asked.

Jim scratched his head. "I can make a request of Southwest, United and Delta to flag his name and contact me if he books a flight out of Santa Fe."

"Great, do it, I think this case is going to head in a different direction for a while." I laid out my theory that maybe the jumper was a tenant, not a guest at Wharf Landing and maybe we already had his name. We just didn't know which name it was.

"We can't search every unit without a warrant and I doubt any judge will issue twenty-four of them without probable cause for each one," Jim said.

We both fell silent while we pondered the dilemma. Then, across the hall, I saw Mike Kelly walking toward his office. "Hey, Captain Kelly, got a minute?" I shouted.

Mike's head turned, saw me waving and came over to Jim's cubicle. "Rick, what's up?" I filled him in on the problem we were facing with Wharf Landing.

"Jim's right," he said. "No judge will issue all those warrants. Got any other ideas?"

I did have another idea, one that I hadn't mentioned to anyone. To make it happen I would have to go through Alex and as I learned early in my career, you don't run an important decision by the police department before running it by her. "None," I answered.

~ * ~

When I got back to my building I headed straight for the third floor and Dr. Alexandra Keller's office. I took my usual seat across the desk from her.

"Wow, twice in two days. Something must be important," she said.

"How's your budget doing this year?" I asked.

"Uh, oh, the last time you asked about my budget I ended up funding a trip to Arkansas for you. Which state are you headed to this time?"

"None."

"Okay, then why are you interested in my budget?"

"I want to go to Bogotá."

"Colombia? Why Colombia?"

"I told you earlier the jumper was carrying a briefcase that was purchased there."

"But you didn't tell me what was in it."

"On advice from the lawyer you sent me to."

"To hell with the lawyer, I can keep a secret. Tell me."

Up jumped the devil—again. I made direct eye contact and said, "Nothing, it was empty."

"I don't believe you."

"Well, that's my story and I'm sticking to it."

"Okay, so what do you expect to find in Colombia?"

"If I can find out the name of the person who bought the briefcase and if that same name is on the Wharf Landing roster, we'll know who our John Doe is."

"Why doesn't Mike Kelly just order a search for an abandoned unit in the building?"

"It's not that easy. He says a judge would never allow it."

Alex had the look of someone who had just eaten a bad piece of fish. "Rick, I'm scared, every time you go on a fact-finding mission you almost get yourself killed."

"I doubt anyone would want to kill me for nosing around a leather goods store."

She stood, walked to the window and stared out. "I

can't take the chance."

"I'll sign a document to release the medical examiner's office of liability."

"Rick, I'm not worried about the liability, I'm worried about you. No, I can't let you go."

"Alex, don't make me beg. It demeans me."

She shook her head. "Okay, okay, I'll fund your escapade, but if you don't make it back, I'll never forgive you."

"I'm just looking for a name, not a nuclear secret."

"I know, but be careful anyway. Please."

"I will. If anyone asks, I'm dealing with a personal issue for a few days."

"Got it. Good luck."

CHAPTER THIRTY

I checked the flights from San Francisco to Bogotá. No carriers flew directly, but if I left at 7:15 the next morning, United had a flight to Bogotá with only an hour and seven-minute layover in Houston. I'd arrive at 7:20 p.m. Colombian time. I booked it on my credit card. Alex would be good for it.

When I stepped into the reception room, Stella was busy at her desk doing whatever she does. She looked up from the computer screen. "Hey, Boss, what's up?"

"I'm taking a little trip for a few days."

"*Ooh la la,* as your French girlfriend might say."

I should never have told Stella about Frankie. "I'm going alone; this one's all business."

"Where to?"

"Can you keep a secret?"

"You know me."

"That's the problem, I do." She touched her index finger to her lips. "Okay," I said. "Bogotá, Colombia."

"Ugh, why?"

"Can't tell you, but if anyone asks where I am, what will you tell them?"

"Uh, let's see. 'Dr. Rose is out of the office this week. May I take a message?'"

"What if the caller asks where I am?"

"Uh, 'Dr. Rose is attending to a personal issue.'"

"Perfect. What if Captain Kelly asks?"

"Dr. Rose is attending to a personal issue."

"Okay, you're on your own for lattes this week. Wish me luck."

"Do you need it?"

"I hope not."

After leaving my office, I stopped at Josie's truck, where she was forcing hot water through the coffee machines. "Can you take care of the monster for another couple of days?" I asked.

"Are you going away with your girlfriend again?"

"Who said I have a girlfriend?"

"News travels fast through a coffee truck."

"I'm going away on business." Her expression said, 'I don't believe you.' I raised my hand as if taking an oath. "Honest."

I called for a taxi and while I waited, I tapped my speed dial to tie up one last loose end. Frankie and I had a date for Friday evening. "*Allô*, Rick, is everything all right?" she asked.

"Fine, why?"

"You don't usually call in the middle of the day."

"I know, but I have to cancel Friday. I'm leaving town on business."

"Oh, for how long?"

"Not long, two, maybe three days at the most. I'll call you as soon as I get home."

"I'll wait for your call and when you get back, instead of going to a restaurant, I want to cook you a real French dinner."

"That would be great. See you in a couple of days."

~ * ~

United makes it easy at Houston's George Bush Intercontinental Airport. Terminal E handles both their domestic and international flights. My flight from San Francisco was a half hour late, but the plane to Bogotá was only three gates away and I boarded it with time to spare.

When I was growing up in Brooklyn, Colombia sounded like it was halfway around the world; actually, it's the most northern country in South America and in a little under five hours, I stepped off a jetway in Bogotá's El Dorado International.

I hate to admit my own ignorance, but I knew nothing about the country. The first thing that struck me was the large number of armed police officers roaming through the airport. They all carried handguns, and a few held larger weapons. Several were leading German Shepherds, who sniffed and smelled everything in their vicinity.

The cab driver spoke passable English and asked where I was going. I had my choice of hotels with exotic Spanish names, but I chose the Bogotá Marriott. Somehow it sounded familiar, safer, and more likely to have soft toilet paper.

It was well after ten o'clock by the time I settled into my room and I was pleasantly surprised. It was larger and better arranged than most of the Marriotts I'd booked in the States. Unpacking took all of three minutes; other than underwear, socks, two shirts and a pair of khakis, all I brought with me was the briefcase the jumper had given to Bruno.

Before showering and getting some needed sleep, I googled the address for Mario Fernández leather goods and a fancy webpage popped up with a mission statement: *We are the luxury that is born from our artisans and their life stories. Our products represent our community and our brand is committed to being the best. We have the privilege of representing a country, the Colombian luxury.*

Uber is international, which includes Bogotá, so the app on my phone worked perfectly. I was confident that even though the address, <u>Cra. 62D #13 - 53, Int 7</u>, made no sense to me, the Uber driver would know where it was. I stored it on the app and fell asleep for eight hours.

Breakfast the next morning was a serendipitous experience. The waiter suggested I have an order of *arepas* along with my cup of Colombian coffee. I had no idea what *arepas* was, but I was delighted when it arrived. On the plate was a cornmeal cake split open and topped with butter, scrambled eggs, cheese, and five slices of avocado. The coffee was served black in a small cup and sweetened with raw sugar.

~ * ~

I was right about the Uber driver knowing the address. He dropped me in front of the store less than ten minutes after leaving the hotel. For a shop that sold $8,000 purses and $10,000 briefcases, it was unassuming. No display windows, no fancy signs, just the name, Mario Fernández, embossed on the front door.

I stepped inside and was immediately greeted by an attractive woman, probably in her early forties, dressed to the nines. *"Buenos días, Señor. ¿Cómo puedo ayudarle?"*

I began with my universal form of communication—a big smile. "Good morning," I said. "English?"

"Sí ... yes, how may I help you?"

I took the briefcase from a brown paper bag and laid it on a display case. "I'm inquiring about this briefcase. Was it purchased here?"

The woman took one look at it and said, "Most definitely. It is the premier item in our store. Whoever purchased this case has excellent taste."

"That's what I'm inquiring about. How would I go about finding the name of the buyer?"

"So, the briefcase, it is not owned by you?"

"I bought it second hand, but it had something of great value left inside it. I'd like to return that to the original owner."

"I'm sorry, sir, you will have to talk to my manager, Señor Pérez Garcia."

While waiting for the saleswoman to locate the manager, I perused the display cases. Everything from purses, handbags, briefcases, shoes and jackets were made from the finest leather. The prices were displayed in Colombian pesos, so I wasn't sure of what the dollar amounts were, but I did notice there were a lot of zeros after the other numbers.

"¿Señor? a voice said.

I turned to face a man sporting the thickest, blackest, mustache I'd ever seen. "Señor Garcia?" I asked.

"Pérez Garcia ... Señor Juan Pérez Garcia. Here in Colombia we take two last names, our father's first surname followed by our mother's first surname."

I felt as though I'd left some breakfast egg on my face. "Oh, so sorry, I didn't know."

"That is no problem. You are an American?"

I offered my hand. "Rick Rose, one first name, one last."

He responded with a firm handshake. "Señorita Rojas Cárdenas tells me you are inquiring as to the buyer of one of our cases that is now in your possession."

"Right, I want to return something I found inside."

"You travelled all the way from America to Colombia just to return this item?"

"No, I'm here on business, so I brought the briefcase with me hoping you could steer me to its buyer."

Señor Juan Pérez Garcia pointed to the countertop where the case was lying. "May I?"

I nodded. He picked it up and after caressing the outside of the leather, he opened it and held it under a table lamp. "You saw our markings inside, did you not?"

"Yes, the name of your business and some sort of postal code."

He motioned for me to take a look and I went closer to the light and peeked inside: *Mario Fernández–Bogotá, CO 23-106.* "That is not a postal code," he said. "Those numbers indicate this briefcase was made in the year 2023 and of this model, it was the one hundred and sixth produced."

"So, with individually numbered cases, you must keep a record of the buyers."

"Perhaps. Please wait here and I'll check." He scurried off in the direction of his office.

To pass the time I approached the saleswoman. "Your manger explained the surname custom in Colombia, but I'm curious. If a woman has two surnames and then marries, does she then have three surnames?"

The woman smiled. "Not exactly. In Colombia a married woman has the choice of taking on her husband's surname. If she chooses to do so, she adds the prefix, *de*, which means 'from.' For example, in my case I might be, Señora Rojas Cárdenas de Torres." I nodded as if I understood, but I didn't have a clue.

Señor Pérez Garcia returned empty-handed. "Sorry, I can't give you the information you seek."

"Why?"

"The head office forbids it."

"Why is that?"

"It appears the case was purchased by a very important person."

"So what?"

"In our country discretion is paramount, lest there be consequences."

"Who did you talk to at the head office?'

He glanced around the room before answering. "Our vice president in charge of sales, Señor Ramírez Díaz."

"Where is your head office located?"

"In Cartagena."

"How far is that from Bogotá?"

"About 650 kilometers." I paused my questioning to do the math. "Four hundred miles," he said.

CHAPTER THIRTY-ONE

The flight to Cartagena took less than an hour. Twenty minutes later I was in a cab heading to the center of the city. Unlike Bogotá, that is built on a plateau in the mountains, Cartagena is at sea level and faces the Caribbean. We passed several neighborhoods where occupants were living in cardboard or corrugated metal shacks, but by the time we reached the Hotel Caribe, in the Bocagrande area, I felt like I was in Miami Beach.

The hotel was ostentatiously lavish. The lobby was built with multicolored Spanish tile and marble columns that reached two stories to the ceiling. Every room in the hotel faced a body of water, either the Caribbean Sea to the west or Cartagena Bay to the east.

A room with a partial view was going for $165, but for another fifty-two bucks, I got one with a panorama of the sea. I snapped a picture with my phone on the expectation that when I showed it to Alex, she would forgive me for overspending.

After tossing my carry-on onto the bed, I took out the briefcase and unfolded the note containing the address for Mario Fernández' head office. When I had asked Señor Pérez Garcia for this address, he had been reluctant to give it to me. He did comply, but not before scanning the room to make sure no one was watching. I thought it was odd but didn't dwell on it. I grabbed the briefcase, typed the address into my Uber app and went down to the lobby to wait for my ride.

"Do you know where this address is?" I asked the driver.

He understood English but only spoke two words and they were both the same. "Yes, yes," he responded.

"Is it far from here?"

"Yes, yes."

"Will it take more than twenty minutes?"

"Yes, yes."

I decided to test his comprehension. "Am I the ugliest guy you've ever seen?"

"Yes, yes, *treinta minutos*."

I expected the Mario Fernández' headquarters to be in an office complex or high-rise, but when the driver pulled to a stop, we were on a street lined with shops and restaurants. Just as it was in Bogotá, there were no display windows, no fancy signs, just their name embossed on the front door. I stepped inside.

A young man dressed in a blazer, slacks and an open white shirt, approached me. *"Buenos días, Señor. ¿Cómo puedo ayudarle?"*

"Speak English?" I asked.

"Yes, sir, how may I help you?"

I reached into my pocket for the note and read the name off it. "Is Señor Ramírez Díaz in?"

"Yes, his office is in the rear of the shop ... and you are ...?"

I dug out my business card, the one with the raised gold medical examiner logo, and handed it to him.

He stared at it and asked the obvious. "May I ask, what

an odontologist is?"

"You can, but it's too complicated to explain. Just tell Señor Ramírez Díaz that I'm from the United States."

He disappeared into a back room, leaving me once again to peruse displays of very expensive leather goods. Whether by necessity or intention, I was kept waiting for almost an hour before the rear door opened and the young man motioned me to follow him. On the other side of the door was a set of stairs. I followed him to the second floor, where he knocked, opened the door and held out his hand, signaling me to step inside.

Sitting behind a large desk was a small man sporting wire spectacles and a pencil thin moustache. His English was impeccable. "Dr. Rose," he held out his hand. "I'm Señor Ramírez Díaz. I have been expecting you."

I shook his hand and took a seat. "Really. News travels fast in Colombia."

"Believe it or not, Dr. Rose, we have had phones here for over a century."

"I apologize, I didn't mean it that way. I assume your Bogotá manager, Señor Juan Pérez Garcia, gave you a heads up."

"Your assumption is correct. Now, what is the real reason you need to know who purchased that case you are carrying?"

"My job is to identify people who have died without identification. This briefcase was in the possession of such a man. You could make my job a lot easier."

He plucked at the thin band of hair over his upper lip. "It is not my job to make your job easier. Tell me, though, how did this man die?"

"I'm afraid that's confidential."

"I see." He gave me a twisted grin. "And so is the name

of the buyer of the briefcase."

"Are you suggesting a trade?"

"I believe I am."

Something about this guy gave me the creeps. Maybe a half-truth was in order. "He committed suicide."

"By a gunshot wound?"

Either this guy was psychic or somebody from the U.S. had already given him the answer. "No," I said. "He jumped off the Golden Gate Bridge." I heard the door open behind me and assuming it was the young man returning, I didn't turn around. The last thing I remember was a tremendous flash of light behind my eyeballs.

I have no idea how long I was unconscious, but it was long enough to dream. I was lying on a lounger, next to the pool at the Hotel Caribe, with a drink in my hand. I knew it was alcohol, something I haven't touched in over four years. The water of the Caribbean was so blue I couldn't tell where it ended and the sky began. I closed my eyes. When I opened them, Frankie was standing over me. She looked beautiful. She wore a bikini that barely covered anything. The rest of her skin was tan and shimmering from the lotion spread across it. "Get up and give me a kiss," she said.

I tried, but I couldn't. I pushed against the lounger, but my body felt like it weighed a thousand pounds. I tried again, and again, and again. "I can't," I said.

"Yes, you can." She curled her finger. "Come with me; I'm leaving."

Somehow, I defied gravity and found myself holding Frankie's hand on the edge of a steep cliff high above the Caribbean. "You love me, don't you," she said.

"Yes, I do."

"You want to be with me forever?"

I squeezed her hand. "I do, forever."

She smiled, kissed me on the lips, and pulled away. "Come with me, then."

"Where? Where are you going?" She looked over the cliff and out to sea. "No, don't," I yelled and reached for her. She jumped.

Drenched in sweat, I opened my eyes, or I should say eye; the left one was swollen shut. Standing over me I saw an ominous looking man holding a wooden club.

CHAPTER THIRTY-TWO

Even with one eye, it didn't take long to assess my situation; it was right out of a gangster movie. I was strapped to a chair with my hands tied behind my back and my ankles bound together. My head was pounding and I could see blood stains down the front of my shirt and across the top of my khakis.

The guy with the club was a mean looking sonofabitch. He was big, he was ugly and he had a scowl that looked like it was a permanent fixture on his face. He must have seen me move and shoved his head up to mine for a closer look. I inhaled the noxious blend of garlic, tobacco and alcohol and turned away. He stepped back and shouted at someone out of my field of vision. "*Él está despierto.*"

An older man, my guess in his middle sixties, stepped in front of me. He was well groomed and wore pants, shirt and a vest that were no doubt parts of a business suit. He clasped his hands together revealing a huge ring, like the one the jumper wore, and a gold watch that looked like it belonged in Fort Knox. "How are you feeling, Dr. Rose?" he asked, like a surgeon who had been called in on a difficult case.

It's hard to shoot a dagger with only one eye but I

tried. "How do think I'm feeling?"

He smiled. "I believe it is improper English to answer a question with a question. Shall we try again? How are you feeling?"

It was obvious that trying to look tough wasn't going to work. "Terrible," I said.

The man turned to the palooka with the bad breath and said, "*Miguel, tres aspirinas, por favor.*" Then he turned back toward me. "Dr. Rose, if I have your promise not to get combative, I will release your restraints."

By now all I wanted was to get out of there without further damage. "Promise," I said. He reached for a wire cutter and snipped the zip ties that were wrapped around my wrists and ankles. "Thanks," I muttered.

Miguel returned with a bottle of water and three aspirins. I swallowed the pills and drained the bottle.

"I apologize for the rough treatment," the man said. "Miguel and I sometimes have communication difficulties. I would like to ask you a few questions and if I get satisfactory answers, you will be sitting by the pool at the Hotel Caribe in an hour. Shall we begin?"

"Yeah, let's get it over with."

He pulled up a chair with the back facing me and straddled it as he sat down to talk. "Where did you get the briefcase?"

"A guy who jumped off the Golden Gate bridge gave it to his cab driver."

"And the cab driver gave it to you?"

"That's right."

"What was in the briefcase?"

"When he gave it to me?"

"Correct."

"Nothing."

"You told the manager in Bogota that you wanted to return its contents."

"That was a lie.'"

"So, there was nothing in it? No money?"

"No, it was empty."

"Did the cab driver remove anything from the briefcase?"

Now I began to sweat and for good reason. "I have no idea what he did with the briefcase before he gave it to me."

"He didn't mention money?"

"Why would he mention money?"

The man raised his index finger. "There you go again, answering a question with a question."

"No, he didn't mention any money. Okay?"

His warm demeanor turned cold. "You realize, I'm not a store manager. If you lie to me, I may kill you."

"I'm not lying to you."

"That briefcase contained a lot of money. If I find that the cab driver took it for himself, he will have to answer to me."

"I'll let him know."

"You do understand my influence stretches well beyond this country."

"I don't know who you are, but I believe you."

"You are sweating, Dr. Rose, is that because you've been lying to me?"

"It's because I'm scared shitless."

"And you should be. Did your police colleagues find another briefcase?"

"In the cab?"

"No, in the process of their investigation."

"I wouldn't know, ask them."

"I'm asking you. Did they find another briefcase?"

"I don't think so, nobody mentioned one."

"When are you leaving our country?"

"As soon as I can pack."

"I think that is a wise decision. I have a request of you."

"What's that?"

"I want you to drop your investigation. The man who jumped from the bridge is best left without a name."

"But, my job ..."

"Your job is not as important as your life."

"So, this not a request, it's a ..."

"... A threat. Have a safe voyage home, Dr. Rose." He began to walk out of the room, then turned and said, "Oh, one more thing. If you hear of another briefcase, you tell me."

"How, I don't even know who you are."

"I'll be in touch," he said, and slammed the door behind him.

It was obvious Miguel spoke no English, so I followed his signals. He held out his hands. I did the same. He bound my wrists with another zip tie, then grabbed a roll of duct tape in one hand and covered his eyes with the other. I closed my eyes and he spread a strip of tape across them. Then he poked me in the back with his club and I shuffled forward with him pushing me in the right direction. I made it down the stairs and out of a door, where I heard a car door open. He nudged me into the back seat, the engine started and the car began to move. I heard Miguel yell from the outside, "*Adiós, Doctor.*"

When the car came to a stop, I recognized the sweet scent of the palm trees growing in front of the Hotel Caribe. The driver cut off the zip ties, ripped off the tape and pushed me out of the car. I was lying on the ground as it drove off.

One of the doormen rushed to me and looked down at my swollen face and bloody clothes. "Sir, you're injured, may I help?"

I reached into my pocket for my room card and along with it discovered my wallet and passport. I handed the card to the doorman. "Just help me to my room and I'll be fine."

I stumbled into the bathroom and for the first time since the abduction saw my face in the mirror. My left eye was purple and completely closed and above it was a two-inch slice where the club had hit me. Dried blood was everywhere.

I heard a knock on my door and snuck up on the peephole to look out. A uniformed hotel employee was standing in the hall. I latched the chain, so the door would only open an inch or two and eased it ajar. "What is it?" I asked.

"Sir, I understand you've had an accident. We have a doctor in the hotel who can take a look at you."

"That would be fine, send him up."

"Can I do anything else for you?"

"Yes, ask the concierge to book me a seat on the first flight to San Francisco."

CHAPTER THIRTY-THREE

The doctor placed eight sutures to close the wound delivered by Miguel's club and then handed me a dozen 10/325 hydrocodone tablets for the pain. He said one at a time should do the job, but after a twenty-minute shower to wash away the afternoon's blood and sweat, I downed two of the pills and slept until the concierge woke me at six a.m. the next morning.

I packed my things, minus the briefcase that was confiscated by my abductor, bought a pair of over-sized sunglasses and an 'I love Cartagena' baseball cap to cover the swelling and the purple skin. Then, I grabbed the first cab that showed up in front of the hotel.

The cabbie was an ex-pat from the United States and was ecstatic to have an American in his back seat. "So, you down here for pleasure or business?" he asked.

I didn't feel like gabbing, but I didn't want to be rude to a countryman either. "Business," I said.

"Yeah, what kind of business?""

I wasn't about to explain the difference between an orthodontist and an odontologist for the umpteenth time, so I answered, "Leather goods."

"Cool, what kind of leather goods?"

"Briefcases, mainly."

"Very, cool. Ya buy 'em or sell 'em?"

In lieu of breakfast, I had popped two pain pills and they were beginning to whack me out. The driver was a good guy, but I couldn't help it, I fell asleep before I could answer another of his questions. I awoke twenty minutes later to the sound of his raspy voice. "Hey, buddy … wake up, we're at the airport."

I guess it wasn't a good idea to ask for the first flight out of Cartagena, it had two layovers: one in Miami and another in Denver. It was well after midnight when I trudged up a jetway in the San Francisco airport.

I didn't sleep well that night. My promise to Bruno and his wife had come back to haunt me again. I was in a lose-lose situation. The suitcase the jumper had given to Bruno contained $250,000 in cash. He and his wife kept the money to pay for their kid's college expenses and I promised not to tell anyone. Now, a Mr. Big in Colombia says if he finds that Bruno kept that money, Bruno's in big trouble. I needed help from my police colleagues, help they couldn't give unless I provided them with the facts. I was hopeful, if I told them, they would pledge secrecy, but if a crime had been committed, I would be exposing them, along with myself to prosecution. I decided, for now, to keep quiet.

After about two hours of sleep, I showered, dressed and put on my hat and sunglasses. It was after nine, but instead of going to my office, I gave the Uber driver the address of Teddy Small Jr., the lawyer Alex had referred to me a couple of weeks ago.

I think his receptionist looked at my beat-up face and took pity on me; in between scheduled clients she squeezed me in.

"You're back," he said. "I'm guessing you have more

concerns about the money."

I told him about my trip to Colombia and I left no details out. "Am I in legal trouble?" I asked.

"That depends on what you do from this point on."

"How so?"

"Okay, until now we didn't know if the source of the money in the guy's briefcase came from criminal activity. Hell, as far as we know it could have come out of his 401K. But now it's starting to sound more like dirty money from Colombia. You ask if you're in trouble? Not if you share all this information with your police colleagues, but ..."

"But what?"

"They'll make the cab driver and his wife surrender the money."

"Oh, man, I can't do that to them. They've already used some of it for college costs."

"I told you at our first meeting there might be a solution to your criminal dilemma, but by its very nature, your ethical one would be unresolvable."

My head was throbbing and it wasn't from being hit with a club. "What if I take my chances and keep the money a secret?"

"Rick you're not thinking straight. Besides exposing yourself to criminal charges, you may need police protection and so may the cab driver and his family. You either fess to the truth about the money or you're all in the Colombian's crosshairs."

I knew he was right, but I was conflicted. I thanked him and left.

~ * ~

It was too late to stop at Josie's, so I had to greet Stella empty-handed. "Sorry, no lattes today."

The color drained from her cheeks. "What happened?"

"Just got up late; she was closed."

"Not the coffee, your face. What happened to it?"

"I took a pee in the middle of the night and walked into a door."

"You used that lie the last time you got yourself beaten up."

"Did I? Did it fly?"

"Not then, not now."

"Okay, I got the shit beat out of me again, but it looks worse than it is."

She held her makeup mirror in front of my face. "I'm sure that's true, it couldn't look much worse."

I took off the sunglasses to look at my reflection. The purple discoloration and swelling around my left eye had succumbed to gravity and had dropped into my cheek and circled the corner of my mouth.

When Stella saw that my eye was swollen shut, she screamed. "My God, it is worse."

"Okay, let's drop it, I have some thinking to do." I went into my private office to meditate.

CHAPTER THIRTY-FOUR

S omething wasn't adding up. Two hundred and fifty thousand dollars is a lot of money to most people, but is it important enough to Mr. Big that he'd kill for it? I saw the guy's jewelry; his gold watch probably cost him a hundred thousand and that fancy ring on his pinky, at least twenty-five. He couldn't be that upset over 250k, so what is he upset about? Whatever it is, it's somehow related to the Jumper.

I kind of dozed off for a few minutes and wasn't sure if the epiphany hit me in a conscious or unconscious state, but now it was clear to me. I called for a cab, grabbed my jacket and stopped at Stella's desk. "Don't tell anyone I'm back yet."

"What? Why?"

"Can't tell you, just say I texted you and said I'd be home tomorrow."

"Okay, you're the boss."

"I don't want anyone in the building to see me here, so I want you to hold the elevator doors open while I make it down the stairs and into the back parking lot."

"You meeting James Bond there?"

"Very funny, let's go."

Stella called the elevator down from the fourth floor.

When the doors opened, she looked inside and after confirming it was empty, pushed the 'hold' button. "Get going," she said.

It took the cabbie less than twenty minutes to get to Ocean Beach, where I pointed out the house. "I'm only going to be a few minutes," I said. "You want to wait?" He threw up his hands as if he had nothing better to do. I jumped out and knocked on Bruno's door.

I wasn't sure if I'd catch him or his wife at home, but as far as I was concerned, either one would do. I was in luck; they both were there. "Dr. Rose, come in," Bruno said.

We sat in the living room where Bruno's wife cautiously joined us. "Is this about the money?" she asked.

I nodded. "I'm afraid it is."

"Is that why your face is a mess?"

"Yes."

"So, you told someone about the money," Bruno said.

"No, someone already knew about it and they don't want you to have it."

"But you promised we could keep it," his wife said.

"I promised you could keep the money for your kid's college costs, but that was before you lied to me."

The blood drained from both their faces. "Wha … what d'ya mean?" Bruno asked.

"There was more than $250,000 in the briefcase, wasn't there?"

"No. Is that what this other person told you?"

"Mr. and Mrs. Cappelletti, there's an old saying, 'be a pig not a hog.' Which are you?"

Bruno's wife was the first to crack. "Dr. Rose, please, we took out a third mortgage on our house. Without the money from the briefcase, we'll lose our home."

"How much?" I asked.

"How much do we owe?"

"No, how much was in the briefcase?"

They both answered at the same time. Bruno blurted out, "Three hundred" while his wife mumbled, "Four-fifty."

"Look, I have a cab waiting, so that gives you about ten seconds to tell me the truth. If you lie to me one more time, all the money is going to the police department."

Bruno's eyes caught those of his wife. In unison they said, "a million."

You could hear the proverbial pin drop until I broke the silence. "Folks, a very bad guy knows about that money and he doesn't want you to have it."

"So, he's the one who messed up your face?" Bruno asked. I nodded.

Bruno's wife began to sob. He went to her and put his arms around her. "It's all right, Maria. I'll pick up an extra shift."

She wiped her eyes on the edge of her apron. "You already work twelve hours a day, six days a week. It will kill you."

Tears began to well in my eyes too. "Look," I said. "Maybe there's a way." I turned to Maria. "Enzo Mancini, Bruno's lawyer, he's your brother. Right?"

"Yes, but ..."

"You get ahold of him and have him meet you and Bruno right away at Captain Kelly's office. Then you pack up $750,000 and take it down there. Bruno, tell him you're sorry. Tell him you were scared to turn the money in earlier for fear gangsters were involved. Tell him it's a load off your conscience. Tell him anything but give him the money. If it gets messy, your brother-in-law can lay some lawyer stuff on him."

Bruno looked stunned. "What about the other $250,000?"

"What other $250,000?"

"Dr. Rose, this guy who beat you up could kill us. You said as much."

"For keeping $1,000,000, yes, but for $250,000 ... probably not. I'm counting on him not being a 'hog.'" Maria came to me and kissed me on the cheek. "Don't get all mushy on me," I said. "Just make sure you get down there today, before Kelly leaves."

When I got back to the cab, the driver was pissed. He pointed at his watch. "You said a few minutes, it's been twenty."

I handed him two tens. "This is for you, off the meter." He smiled and dropped me at my house fifteen minutes later. It was lonely without my little buddy. He was a pain in the ass, but he was a good companion. I hit my speed dial.

"*Allô*, Rick, you're back."

"For you I am, for everyone else I'll be home tomorrow."

"I feel special."

"You are special. How about that dinner tonight?"

"I'll have it in the oven by six. See you then."

CHAPTER THIRTY-FIVE

Frankie answered the door wearing a lot more than she wore in my dream but still looking radiant. For my liking, natural beauty always trumps a made-up version and tonight all Frankie wore on her face was a smile and a light gloss on her lips. I bent down and kissed them.

"Well, well, where did that come from?" she said.

"From a man who missed you."

She stepped back to get a better look at me. "Rick, what happened?"

I didn't really have a pat answer to that question. I'd told Stella I walked into a door, but that didn't fly, so I figured when all else fails, the truth would have to do. "I got the crap beat out of me."

She gingerly caressed my swollen cheek. "Oh, Rick, I'm so sorry. Care to talk about it?"

"You wore a bikini."

"I what?"

"When I was out cold, I dreamed of you in a bikini."

"Really. How did I look?"

"Like a swimsuit model."

"Have you ever been to a beach in France?"

"Only through *National Geographic* when I was thirteen years old."

"So, you know that the bikini is out and the monokini is in."

"Yeah, what's next? A cork and two pasties?"

She broke out laughing. "Come, I have a bottle of 2022, French Bloom La Cuvee."

"Frankie, I can't."

"Yes, you can. This is an alcohol-free sparkling wine made from organic chardonnay grapes. I challenge you to recognize it from authentic champagne."

Frankie led me to the couch where the bottle of wine along with two champagne flutes were set out. She filled the glasses and we tapped them together. "To a beautiful scar over your eye," she said.

"Yeah, I'm not looking forward to that."

"*Au contraire, mon ami*, it is very sexy when worn on a handsome man." She wrapped her arm around mine and we drank from each other's glass.

"Wow, are you sure there's no alcohol in this?" I asked.

"No alcohol, no buzz and no hangover."

We killed the bottle and sat down for dinner. It was vintage French. Frankie's salad was a simple blend of butter lettuce, a dusting of oil and vinegar and fresh ground pepper. When she served her main course, she dished it from a copper pot onto antique porcelain plates.

"Delicious," I said. "I know I had this once at a little restaurant in the West Village of New York."

"*Oui, c'est Coq au vin* from the Burgundy region of France. It's nothing more than a stew made of chicken braised with wine, lardons, mushrooms, and garlic."

"I love it … uh, what are lardons?"

"Small pieces of bacon. You know, in English, bacon and lard are connected. Yes?"

We sat for a few minutes, not speaking, just enjoying each other's company. Frankie broke the trance. "I have two desserts for you tonight. One is from the kitchen, the other is not. Which do want first?"

I grinned. "How about the other one."

The souffle we ate later was luscious, but it couldn't hold a candle to the first dessert. By midnight I was barely able to keep my eyes open.

"Do you want to stay over?" Frankie asked.

"Raincheck? I need my own bed."

She kissed me. "Understood. I'm just glad you're home."

~ * ~

The next day I slept in until ten, dressed, had coffee, and then took the cable car to work. It was close to noon by the time I got to my office.

"Are you home from Colombia yet?" Stella asked.

I chuckled. "Yeah, got off the plane an hour ago."

"Good. Captain Kelly's been calling all morning."

"I figured that. Call his secretary and make an appointment for this afternoon. I'm headed up to Alex' office."

Alex took one look at me and covered her eyes with her hand. "Not again," she said.

"It's not that bad."

"It will be 'not that bad' when your left eye opens again. Right now, it's very bad. "Who did it?"

"A guy who wasn't happy that the briefcase I brought down to Colombia was empty."

"I don't get it, what did this guy expect?"

This was a big moment. Pandora's box, or more appropriately, the jumper's briefcase, opened yesterday afternoon when Bruno turned $750,000 over to Mike

Kelly. Now I could tell Alex the truth. Well, not 'the whole truth and nothing but the truth' but at least part of it. "This guy expected a briefcase full of money, but Bruno and his wife emptied it."

"So, that was the big secret you couldn't tell me?"

"That was it."

"Why are you telling me now?"

"Because, if I'm not mistaken, yesterday Bruno turned $750,000 over to Mike Kelly."

"And why does this Colombian guy think it's his?"

"He didn't say it was his, but he said it wasn't Bruno's."

"So, do you think the jumper worked for him?"

"Maybe, maybe not. When we find out how the jumper came in possession of the briefcase, we'll know the answer to that question."

"Quite a story."

"That's not all."

"What else?"

"The Colombian guy threatened to kill me if I don't drop the jumper case."

Alex slumped into a chair like her heart had skipped a beat. "Rick, I'm taking you off this case. You didn't sign up for this when I hired you."

"No, I didn't, but being off the case isn't going to stop our Colombian friend, so I have to stick it out. I'm going to ID the jumper and when I do, Mr. Big will realize that Mike Kelly has the contents of the briefcase. I will be of no value to him."

"What if he doesn't see it that way?"

"Then you'll be short one forensic odontologist."

"Rick, I'm scared, what can I do?"

"Just stop worrying."

CHAPTER THIRTY-SIX

When I stepped into Mike Kelly's office, he and Jim were laughing it up, probably from one of Jim's chauvinistic jokes. When I first met Jim, he was a card-carrying misogynist, but he's reformed ... well, sort of. He was the first to spot me. "Holy, shit, what's the other guy look like?"

"Like a rich guy who has someone else do his dirty work."

Mike patted a chair seat and I joined them at a conference table. "So, I hear you went to Colombia. Was that guy part of the welcoming committee?" he asked.

"No, he showed up later. I traced the briefcase to where it was purchased in Bogotá and they had a record of the buyer, but they wouldn't divulge his name to me. When I got too nosy, I got cold cocked and woke up tied to a chair in an empty warehouse somewhere."

"Is he the guy who bought the briefcase?"

"I assume so; he knew all about it."

"Did you give it back to him?"

"Didn't have to, he confiscated it."

"Why?"

Now was the time to tell the truth but leave out the part about college money. "He implied that the last time he saw the briefcase it contained a lot of money."

"Did he say how much?"

"No, but he inferred when he finds out who took it, he'll kill them."

Mike looked at Jim and Jim returned the look. Mike said, "Rick, while you were away, the cab driver came into the station and handed me $750,000. He said it was in the briefcase when the jumper gave it to him."

"Did he say why he kept it a secret?"

"He was all over the place, talking about gangsters and hitmen and all sorts of gibberish. His lawyer finally stepped in and said the guy just panicked, but since he eventually did the right thing, he pleaded for us to give the guy a pass."

"And?"

"Yeah, we slapped his hand and sent him home."

"Mike, what happens to the money that was in the briefcase when this investigation is over?"

"Depends."

"On?"

"Whether someone can rightfully claim it."

"And if they can't?"

"Split it up among local charities, most likely."

"What about my guy in Colombia."

"I doubt he'll be able to claim it. Too many questions to answer."

That made me uneasy, but so long as Mr. Big thought the police had the entire $1,000,000, the Cappellettis and I would be safe. I had one more question for Mike. "Have you turned up anything on a second briefcase?"

"Second briefcase? No, why?"

"It's probably nothing. Let me know if you do."

Jim, who had been quiet during the conversation,

spoke up. "About an hour ago I got a call from my United guy in Santa Fe. Hans Van den Brink booked a flight to Acapulco."

"No kidding, what are you going to do?"

"His flight's a red eye." He looked at his watch. "If we leave soon, we can get there in time to pick him up before it takes off."

~ * ~

Jim and I caught a 6:30 flight out of San Francisco that had an hour and twenty-minute layover in Phoenix. With the one-hour time change, we landed in Santa Fe a little before 11:00. Hans' flight to Mexico wasn't scheduled to leave until 12:05.

I thought we'd have plenty of time. What I didn't realize was that even a cop can't run through airport security and onto an airplane without permission. "We have to check in with the airport police," Jim said. "I hate those jerks."

"Why?" I asked.

"They think they're real cops."

"Aren't they?"

"Well, technically, but most of 'em think arresting a shoplifter in the gift store is like solving a major crime."

At this time of night, the chief and captain were long gone. The officer in charge was a lieutenant—a guy named Grady O'Sullivan. After Jim spent ten minutes briefing him, Grady had a glazed over expression. "So, tell me again why you're after this man," he said.

I recognized the look on Jim's face. It usually appears just before he explodes. "What difference does it make? We're after him."

O'Sullivan looked indignant. "It's my job to keep you street cops in check when you're on our turf."

"Turf? What is this, a football field? Just check us in, asshole, our guy's plane leaves in ..." He looked at his watch "... twenty minutes."

If the lieutenant could have moved any slower, he'd have come to a complete stop. Finally, he slid a printed form in front of Jim. "Two initials, sign at the bottom."

Jim spread some chicken scratches across the page, snatched the carbon copy, and we took off. "We need to make one more stop," he said.

"You're kidding."

"TSA. Just to let 'em know I'm carrying a weapon."

By the time we reached the gate, the agent was wrapping up her paperwork. Jim held up his authorization form. "Are all the passengers seated?" he asked.

"Yes, sir, we have a full plane tonight."

"Do you have the passenger manifest handy?" She opened a folder and handed Jim a list of names and seat numbers. He ran his finger down the list and handed it back. "Thanks," he said.

We hustled down the jetway and Jim once again showed the paperwork to a flight attendant, who was getting ready to close the door of the plane. "We need to take a guy off," Jim said.

She stepped aside. "Don't be too long, the captain will have a fit."

"What seat?" I asked Jim.

"42A."

Just as the gate agent said, the flight was jam packed and people were clicking seat belts anxiously waiting to get into the air. When the captain announced a short delay and we walked down the aisle, we weren't met with any smiles. The empty seat stood out. I looked at Jim and he looked at the rear of the plane.

One of the lavatory lights was green, the other was bright red. Jim knocked on the door without getting a reply. "Hans," he shouted. "We know you're in there." When he still didn't get a response, he yelled, "I'll kick this door in if I have to." The door slowly folded open and sitting on the closed toilet lid was my least favorite crypto currency broker.

~ * ~

We landed back in SFO at 7:30 a.m. Jim picked up his Chevy from the police parking lot and we piled in. The ride from the airport to the city started out as a quiet one. Jim looked into his mirror to check on our passenger and said in a raised voice, "You lied to me, pal, you promised not to skip." Hans didn't answer. "Hey, I'm talking to you. You lied to me." Hans remained mute. "Okay, buddy, where do I drop you, Wharf Landing or city jail?"

Apparently, that got Hans' attention. "I didn't skip, I went on vacation."

Jim smirked. "Vacation from what? You don't work."

"What do you want from me?"

"It's not only what I want, it's what I'm going to get. Congratulations, you just earned yourself a spot on the police CI list."

"What's a CI?"

"Confidential informant."

"A snitch?"

"Now, you're catching on. Did your unit at Wharf Landing change hands yet?"

"Not yet."

"Good, you're going to live in it for a while and you're going to keep your eyes and ears open. If you get us the information we want, you're off both our lists."

"Both?"

"Yeah, our CI list and our shit list."

CHAPTER THIRTY-SEVEN

S ince my divorce, I'd only had one serious relationship. I fell in love with a woman who was involved in one of my cases. It didn't end well. She disappeared in the middle of the night leaving behind a note that was delivered to me the next morning. I didn't blame her, I just missed her. Finding Frankie was a godsend, but I didn't want to get hurt again. At age forty, I was afraid to fall in love.

I decided to call my matchmaker, my neighbor, Jacques Devereaux. He picked up on the first ring. *"Bonjour, Docteur Rick*, why the call in the middle of the afternoon?"

"I want to buy you dinner."

"Uh, oh, this is not good."

"I need advice."

"I'm paid $350 an hour for that."

"We'll do a tradeoff. Your professional advice for my professional care."

"But you don't have an office anymore."

"Yes, I do, right above the morgue."

"The morgue is not a dental office."

"No, but if you get murdered, I'll identify you. Deal?"

"Meet you at Frascati around seven."

"You going to be late again?"

"Probably."

"Then let's make it seven-thirty."

"No, seven is good. *Au revoir.*"

~ * ~

Following my return from Colombia, Einstein had been extra schizy. He'd follow me from room to room, never letting me out of his sight, then suddenly he'd disappear, only coming out in the middle of the night to empty his dish. It occurred to me that maybe he should be the one to have dinner with the psychiatrist. I left him a full can of chicken liver pâté and headed out.

Matteo gave me our usual table in the corner. "We have a new beer," he said. "O'Doul's Amber. No alcohol, but in a frozen mug it tastes like an IPA."

I gave him a thumbs up and he had the waiter bring one to my table. I nursed it for twenty-five minutes until 'you know who' showed up. There was no point in scolding Jacques; he loved confrontation. "Perfect timing," I said. "Just got here myself."

He ordered another French meal in an Italian restaurant, but for dessert he condescended and went for an espresso and biscotti. "I am ready now," he said.

"How well do you know Frankie?" I asked.

"Not that well, mainly from studying together at the Sorbonne. I was three years ahead of her."

"Do you know who her family is?"

"Not really, she told me her father works at a bank." I broke out laughing. "What?" he said.

"He owns the Banque de France."

"Really, if I had known, I would have dated her myself instead of fixing her up with you. So, her family, is this a problem for you?"

"Sort of. I grew up in an apartment in Brooklyn and she grew up in a chateau near Versailles."

Jacques' flippant persona transformed into his professional one. "Rick, do you care for this woman?"

"Yeah, I do, but ..."

"But you're intimidated."

"I am, sorta. I love being with her and I know she feels the same about me, but our backgrounds are so far apart."

"I sense there is something else."

Now I know why people are uncomfortable talking to psychiatrists, they see directly into your soul. "Jacques, she's so smart."

"Does she diminish your intellect?"

"No, just the opposite, she builds me up."

"And this makes you uncomfortable?"

"I'm not sure I deserve it."

"Why is that?"

"I haven't done much with my life."

Jacques rarely showed a judgmental expression, but he shook his head in what looked like frustration. "Are you educated?"

"What d'ya mean?"

"Do you have any educational degrees?"

"Of course."

"What are they?"

"A bachelor of science in biology from NYU and a doctor of dental surgery from UCLA."

"And how long did you study for those?"

"Total?"

"Yes, how many years out of your life?"

"Eight."

"And now you're a forensic odontologist. How many of those are there in the United States?"

"I don't know … maybe a hundred."

"You're right, Rick, you haven't done much with your life."

"Okay, I get it, I get it."

I'm sure if I were in his office, I'd be looking up at him from a couch, but instead I was staring at him across an Italian dinner table.

"Look," he said. "If your dissimilar socio-economic backgrounds are too much for you to handle, you have a valid concern, but don't talk yourself out of this relationship on the grounds that Frankie is too smart for you. That just is not true."

"Thanks, my friend, I'll think about that. Say, on a non-professional subject, I have a question for you."

"I'm completely ears."

"All ears, the saying is 'I'm all ears.'"

"Fine, I'm all ears then."

"When you took Adriana Vargas out for dinner, where did you pick her up?"

"Wharf Landing, of course."

"Why where she works? Why not where she lives?"

"That is where she lives."

"Come on, I saw the list of Wharf Landing owners and her name wasn't one of them."

"Well, I'm sorry to burst your bubble, dear boy, but she does lives there. As a matter of fact, I spent a wonderful night in her apartment."

"Which apartment?"

"I was quite drunk, but I believe it was one of the penthouses on the top floor. Why is this so important to you?"

"I'm not sure it is, at least not yet."

~ * ~

As soon as I got home, I searched my desk for the list of Wharf Landing owners that Adriana Vargas had given to Jim. I couldn't find it and remembered I left it in my office desk drawer. I tried to picture it. It wasn't a long list, twenty-four if I recall correctly. It didn't make sense. I knew Adriana wasn't one of them.

Maybe it was the stress of the case or maybe it was the emotional trauma from my psychiatric session, but I was beat. I stored the conundrum somewhere in my brain and fell asleep at my desk.

I woke abruptly. It was four in the morning. I think I had the answer.

CHAPTER THIRTY-EIGHT

The line in front of Josie's Java truck was unusually long this morning. It took me almost fifteen minutes to reach the order window, where my stressed ex-wife was splitting her time between the coffee machines and the customers. "Hi, Rick, I see your face is healing up."

"Yeah, it's doing good." I looked behind me. At least ten people were still waiting their turn. "This is too much work for one person. Maybe it's time you hire a helper," I said.

"You think? I'd like to, but labor is so expensive."

"Not as expensive as keeping people waiting. I bet for fifteen dollars an hour you could cut down the line and double your gross."

"You really think so?"

"I'm sure of it."

"What about employee benefits?"

"Part time employees don't get benefits."

"Really. Okay, I'll look on Angie's List tonight." She turned her head to peek around me for a glimpse at the queue. "Uh, oh, I better get going. You want the usual today?"

"Yeah, but add a surprise for Stella, she'll love it."

I was right. When Stella took her first sip she grinned. "Yummy, it tastes like an Almond Joy candy bar."

"Close, it's toasted coconut mixed in with almond milk."

Stella ran her tongue over her upper lip and licked off a layer. "Rick, how did I end up with you as my boss?"

"I guess all the good ones were taken."

"Get serious. Will I have this job forever?"

"Forever's a long time, but you'll have it as long as I have mine."

She kissed my cheek. "Thanks, Boss, that's close enough."

We finished our drinks, Stella went back to her computer, and I stepped into my private office to check out my middle-of-the-night epiphany.

I took the Wharf Landing owner's list from my top drawer and examined it. There were no living units on the first floor; it made up the lobby, the administrative office and two restrooms. The second, third, fourth, fifth and sixth floor housed the apartments. But it was the sixth floor, the penthouse floor, that interested me. The list showed only four owners on that floor. The math was simple. Google described Wharf Landing as a twenty-five-unit condominium complex, which meant each of the five residential floors have five units on it. The list of owners that Adriana Vargas gave to Jim showed only four owners on the sixth floor. If Jacques memory was correct, it was the sixth floor where he spent the night in Adriana's apartment. Adriana Vargas left, not only her name, but also her apartment, off the list.

I hailed a cab and had the driver drop me at the police station. Jim was sitting on the edge of a secretary's desk, most likely feeding her a line of B.S. to finagle a date. I interrupted his delivery. "Jim, got a minute?"

He turned, looking annoyed. "Oh, hey, Rick, I was just telling Debbie here about the wild time you and I had last year while we were working your case in Arkansas."

"Yeah, you saved my butt."

A smug smile filled Jim's face. "All in the line of duty. So, what brings you by?"

"I have to talk to you and Mike. Is he around?"

"Was five minutes ago. Let's head to his office." I started down the hall and heard Jim whisper. "Pick you up at eight."

Mike Kelly, as usual, was wearing a perfectly pressed uniform, starched white shirt, and spit-shined shoes. "Sit, guys, I hope you have some good news about our murdered John Doe."

"I have news," I said. "Time will tell if it's good or bad."

"Let's have it," Mike said.

"Adriana Vargas left one apartment and one name off that owner list she gave to Jim."

Jim was startled out of the daydream he was probably having about tonight's tryst. "No shit? Which?"

"Hers. She must live in unit #605."

"Why keep it a secret?" Mike said.

"I don't know, but we'll find out. That might explain why the doorman lied about not seeing the jumper come out of Wharf Landing at three in the morning."

"His boss, who lives on the sixth floor, told him to," Jim said. "You think she shot the jumper?"

I wasn't sure what I thought. Adriana Vargas didn't fit my profile of a killer, but I didn't really know what a killer's profile looked like. "If she didn't, she probably knows who did," I said.

Jim looked at Mike. "Should I pick her up?"

"My gut feeling is to wait," he said. He looked in my direction, which I assumed was for my input.

"I don't think we should tip our hand either. We have a CI in the building; let's put him to work."

Mike looked at Jim. "We have an informant inside?"

"Yeah, sorry, Boss, I forgot to mention it to you. We managed to bring that Hans guy back from Santa Fe."

Mike didn't look happy. I knew Jim was in for a one-on-one with him and I knew it wouldn't be good for Jim. "It was my fault," I said. "I suggested we surprise you when we got some good intel from him."

I'm not a very good liar and I'm sure Mike knew it, but for his own reasons he decided to accept my explanation. "Okay, squeeze this guy. Hard."

~ * ~

Normally, at the station, a meeting with someone who's not a suspect in a crime would take place in the reception room, a cozy environment decorated with pictures and pastels. Jim decided not to use that one. Instead he chose the Bullpen, the drab cubicle housing only a metal table and a few metal chairs. He set the thermostat at eighty-seven degrees.

The receptionist buzzed Jim to tell him Hans Van den Brink showed up for his appointment fifteen minutes early and she seated him in the Bullpen. Jim looked at his watch and smirked. "Come on," he said to me. "Let's get a cup of coffee."

"Now?"

"Yeah, let him sweat a little."

The coffee was standard police issue. The pot looked like it hadn't been washed in twenty years and the mugs looked like they hadn't been rinsed in a week. Jim poured some sticky, syrupy, sludge into a cup. "Sugar? Cream?"

I took another look. "Two sugars and lots of cream."

He handed me the mug. "So, what do we want from this guy?"

"Anything he can find about the tenants in the building, especially Adriana Vargas." I took a sip from my mug and spit it out. "Jeez, Jim, this is cold."

He glanced over at the pot and gave me a sheepish look. "Oh, sorry, someone unplugged it." He looked at his watch. "Let's go, he should be pretty toasty by now."

Jim was right. It was chilly outdoors so Hans was wearing a turtleneck covered by a wool Pendelton. The poor guy looked like a dog who had just clawed his way out of a swimming pool. When he saw us, he pointed to the thermostat. "Can you turn down the heat in here?"

"Sure," Jim said. He unlocked the cover to the controls and turned the thermostat up to ninety-two. Then we sat down facing our confidential informant. "So, how well do you know your fellow owners at Wharf Landing?" Jim asked.

Hans shrugged. "Just enough to say hello in the elevator."

"You must know some of them better than that. Ever been in one of their apartments?"

"Well, yeah, a couple of them."

"What's a couple? Two? Five?"

Hans wiped the sleeve of his shirt across his upper lip. "Yeah, two, I guess."

Jim grabbed a bottle of water from a corner cooler, took a big gulp and handed it to me for a swig. "So, Hans, any of those owners that you know come from Colombia?"

"Yeah, I think so."

"How many?"

"All of them."

"Any idea how they ended up at Wharf Landing?"

"I think Adriana had something to do with it."

My interest piqued. "Adriana? You're on a first name basis with Ms. Vargas?"

"Yeah, a lot of owners are."

"How well do you know her?"

"Not very well."

I had a flashback to Jacques' first and only date with Adriana Vargas. "Ever spend the night in her apartment?" I asked.

"What? What kind of question is that?"

"Answer it," Jim said.

"Once."

"Tell us about her."

"I hardly know her. We had dinner, a roll in the hay, and that was it."

"What country is she from?" I asked.

"I dunno, somewhere in South America. My hormones were acting up, so I wasn't paying much attention to the conversation."

"Did she say she's from Colombia?"

"Maybe." He pulled off his sweater. "Shit, it's hot in here."

"What does maybe mean?" Jim said.

"A lot of the owners are Colombian, maybe she is too. Hey, can I have a bottle of that water?"

Jim slammed the cooler top shut. "Sorry, I took the last one. So … Colombia."

"Yeah, I think she mentioned something about being from there …. or maybe not … hell, I don't remember."

Jim plucked another bottle from the cooler and downed half of it in one gulp. "Did Adriana shoot that guy on August 22nd?" he asked.

"How would I know? One night doesn't make us best friends."

"Okay, I have an assignment for you. I want you to find out more about Adriana Vargas."

"Like what?"

"Like, did she know the guy that was shot."

"How? How can I do that?"

"Hey, you're a con man, you'll find a way."

"But she doesn't even like me."

I held up both hands. "Whoa, you said you spent the night with her."

Hans used his sweater to wipe some sweat from his forehead. "She ... she told me to get lost. Said I ..."

"What?"

"Said I was selfish in the sack."

Jim laughed. "Okay, you have three days to patch up your relationship and bring us something about her. I don't want any excuses, I don't want any whining. You get us something and it better be good or I'm going to charge you with fraud and larceny against Dr. Rose's ex. You got that?" Hans mumbled something unintelligible. "What did you say?" Jim shouted.

"Yeah, I got it."

CHAPTER THIRTY-NINE

I decided to walk back to my office and as much as I hated seeing people with phones glued to their ears, I tapped my voicemail icon and became one of those people. The first message came through the speaker. *"Dr. Rose, this is Rebecca Halifax from Sotheby's International. I'd like to talk to you about the unit I showed you at Wharf Landing."* The second message was similar. *"Dr. Rose, Rebecca Halifax again, I have some updated information about Wharf Landing. Give me a call when you can."*

I checked the time, returned her call and told her I was free for lunch, if that worked for her. We agreed on one-thirty at Sam's Grill, a restaurant in the financial district that dates back to the days of the Gold Rush.

Rebecca was dressed in heels, a pantsuit, and shawl. I had decided to forego my impersonation of a wealthy investor and showed up in my work clothes—loafers, khakis and a turtleneck. She didn't seem to notice.

The lunch crowd was clearing out by the time we arrived and most of the sought-after wooden booths with draw curtains were available. We took a small one in the back of the dining room. Rebecca ordered a glass of chardonnay; I asked for a diet Pepsi.

After a few minutes of small talk, I addressed the

point of our lunch. "So, what's the news on Wharf Landing?'

"The unit you looked at on the second floor has been sold."

"Really, when does it close?"

"Not for a couple of weeks. The owner is back in town and wants access until the first."

Our drinks arrived and we ordered lunch. Rebecca chose a Shrimp Louie and I got a serving of Crispy Calamari.

"So, I guess I'm out of luck," I said.

"Actually, not. It's a bit more expensive, but an apartment on the sixth floor just came on the market."

"The penthouse floor."

"Yes, one of the most sought-after units, 603."

Unit 603 sounded familiar. Why did it ring a bell? And then I had an 'ah ha' moment. "The managing director owns 605, the one two doors away."

"You mean Adriana Vargas."

"Yes."

"Well, she lives there, but she doesn't own it."

"What? Who does?"

"The same person who owns 603 and 604. A man named Emiliano Muñoz."

Our lunch arrived, but my excitement had squelched my appetite. I moved the calamari around the plate, taking a bite now and then. When the bill arrived, we both reached for it. "I wouldn't hear of it," Rebecca said. "Sotheby's is picking up the tab."

It was bad enough that I was wasting her time by using her to glean information, I wasn't about to mooch a meal from her too. I grabbed the check and slid my Visa underneath it. "You can get the next one," I said.

I should have given Rebecca credit for being nobody's fool. "Will there be a next one?" she asked.

"I don't think so."

"Why is that?"

"I'm a fraud, Rebecca. I have neither the inclination nor the means to buy a place at Wharf Landing."

"Rick, I know that."

"You do?"

"We have Equifax run a report on every prospective buyer. You're doing well working for the medical examiner, but not well enough for a condo at Wharf Landing."

So much for my charade with a Mercedes and a chauffeur. "So, why the lunch?"

"I wanted to get to know you better."

"I'm flattered," I said. "But I'm in a serious relationship."

"How serious?"

"Serious enough not to be your guest for lunch."

She shook her head. "I understand. Can't blame a girl for trying."

CHAPTER FORTY

I called Frankie twice the next day and both went to voicemail. I left another message. *"Frankie, I've called several times, are you angry with Me? Please call me back."*

My intercom buzzed and Stella's voice resonated through the speaker. "Boss, you don't look so good this morning, are you okay?"

"Not really."

"You want to talk about it?"

"Sure, I'll take you to lunch."

I've mentioned before that my all-time favorite place for lunch is MoMo's. But Stella had broken up with Maverick, and I didn't want to put her in an uncomfortable spot. She must have read my thoughts. "It's okay if you want to go to MoMo's," she said. "Maverick and I are still friends."

He saw us come through the door and pointed to the end of the bar where my usual stools were unoccupied. In the few seconds it took for us to reach them, he had water and coasters set for us. "Hey Doc ... hey good lookin', it's been a while."

Maverick's wide smile and Stella's pink cheeks told me there was more than a friendship operating here. "You guys catch up," I said. "I have to use the men's room."

I figured five minutes wasn't enough and ten was too many, so I checked my watch and came back in eight. Stella's rosy cheeks were back to normal and she grinned when I sat down. "Guess what?" she said.

I scratched the top of my head. "Uh, let me think … you have a date tonight."

"That obvious, huh?"

"Yeah."

"Well, while Maverick gets us a couple of burgers, tell me what's bothering you."

"I must have done something to upset Frankie. She's not returning my calls."

"You didn't two-time her, did you?"

"No, never."

"Were you with another woman?"

"Yeah, on a business lunch."

"Is she pretty?"

"Yes, but that's not why I went to lunch."

"Maybe Frankie saw you and got the wrong message."

"She's too smart to be upset over a lunch. Maybe I should phone her again."

"No, don't do that. She knows your number. If she wants to call she will."

The food arrived, but I only picked at it. On the way back to the office my phone buzzed. I thought it might be Frankie and answered as quickly as I could. "Rick, it's Jim, our boy Hans has something for us. Can you be here in a half an hour?"

~ * ~

This time the secretary didn't direct me to the ninety-two-degree Bullpen, she pointed to the cozy seventy-degree interview room. When I stepped in, Jim and Hans were lounging in upholstered chairs, drinking coffee and eating donuts. "Pull up a chair," Jim said. He pointed to an open pastry box. "Glazed or jelly?"

I wasn't in the mood for a sugar high and took a seat. I turned to Hans. "So, Detective Allen said you have some information for us about Adriana Vargas."

He handed me his phone. "Tap my photos," he said.

I did as he asked and a photo of Adriana alongside nine men filled the screen. The entire group was holding their right hands over their hearts as though they were pledging allegiance to something or someone. "Where did you get this?" I asked.

"I told Adriana I was traveling to South America and asked if she could give me some pointers. She invited me in and when she went to make coffee, I spotted this picture on her end- table. I snapped a photo of it."

"Why? What's so special about it?"

"I recognized those guys from Wharf Landing. They're all Colombians."

I swiped two fingers across the screen to zoom in and my jaw almost dropped. I pointed at the photo. "Do you recognize these two men?"

Hans took a peek. "No, but I do all the others."

I handed him our phones. "Text this photo to us," I said. While he tapped keys, I looked over at Jim, pointed at Hans and then at the door. Jim nodded.

As soon as Hans finished sending us the photo, Jim stood up and slapped him on the back. "That's good work. We'll be in touch."

Hans looked bewildered. "I brought you what you asked, am I done?"

Jim opened the door and waved him out. "We'll see, stay in touch." As soon as he closed the door, Jim turned to me. "What did you find?"

I pointed to his phone. "Transfer the photo to your computer."

I don't know where the police department got the money, but each detective had a brand-new iMac on their desk. We huddled next to Jim's while he transferred the photo and brought it up on his twenty-four-inch screen.

I pointed to one of the faces. "That's the guy who had me kidnapped in Colombia."

"You sure?"

"I wouldn't forget that face. Zoom in on his little finger."

Jim placed the cursor over it and tapped the plus key a few times. "That's a big ring," he said.

"That's the same ring Helmut took off the jumper."

Jim panned out on the image. "Look, they're all wearing those rings."

I ran my finger across the screen. "Except for Adriana."

"A fraternity, maybe?" Jim said.

"I don't know, I was in a college fraternity and we didn't have anything that looked like those."

"Not all fraternities are college ones. Hey, you asked Hans if he knew your kidnapper, who's the other guy you asked him about?"

I pointed to the man standing next to Mr. Big. "He looks a lot different in this photo than when I met him in the morgue, but if I'm not mistaken … he's the jumper."

CHAPTER FORTY-ONE

S ometimes when I'm working on a difficult case, it helps to take some quiet time just to think. That's what I was doing when my phone buzzed. I checked the ID. "Helmut, what's up?"

"Just got the report from ballistics."

"And?"

"They were able to identify the pistol by the rifling impressions on the bullet."

"Rifling? What's rifling?"

"They're spiral grooves cut into the bullet as it travels through the barrel."

"Okay, so what kind of pistol killed our guy?"

"Ever hear of a 9mm INDUMIL Córdova?"

"No, but I'm not a gun guy so ..."

"I googled it. INDUMIL is a Colombian acronym for *Industria Militar*."

"Militar? Like military?"

"Exactly. INDUMIL is the state-owned arms factory."

"So, this is a military weapon?"

"Sounds like it."

I thanked Helmut, hung up and thought about what he had just told me. Although combat weapons often fall into the hands of civilians, there's a good possibility our jumper was killed by someone from the Colombian military. Why? Why come all the way from Colombia to kill a guy at Wharf Landing?

~ * ~

Adriana Vargas' secretary told me Adriana could be tied up in a meeting for the next hour or two. I said I'd wait and plopped into a seat in the reception room. No one came out of the office during the first hour, but halfway into the second, Adriana opened the door and met me with an icy stare. "What are you doing here, Dr. Rose?"

"Just waiting for your meeting to finish, so we can talk."

"It was cancelled. You can come in now."

I followed her into her office, where from behind her desk, she took a seat that was six inches higher than the one she offered me. "I've heard that controlling the high ground makes it easier to direct fire at the enemy?" I said.

She smiled. "Really? I thought it just made it harder for the enemy to attack uphill. I ask again, what do you want, Dr. Rose?"

"Why did you leave your name off the list that you gave Detective Allen?"

"Because it didn't belong there."

"How do you figure that?"

"Detective Allen asked for a list of owners. I'm not an owner."

"But you are a tenant."

"I'm not an owner. If the detective had asked for a tenant list, my name would have been on it."

"Why didn't you tell us that a man named Emiliano Muñoz owns the unit you live in?"

"You asked for a list of all the owners. Mr. Muñoz is on that list."

"Who is Emiliano Muñoz?"

"I don't understand the question. He's one of the owners of Wharf Landing."

"He must be something more than that. Is he from Colombia?"

"I've told you before, Dr. Rose, asking where our owners are from is not only xenophobic, it is none of your business."

"You forget, Ms. Vargas, that a man was shot in Wharf Landing on August 22nd and died later that night. Everything about this place is my business."

"You don't work for the police force; you work for the medical examiner."

"Would you rather I bring a police officer with me when I visit? Detective Allen is known for being a hard ass."

"What do you want to know?"

"Who's Emiliano Muñoz?"

"He's a retired businessman from Bogotá."

"What kind of business?"

"I never asked him."

"Weren't you curious how he could afford not one, but three units in Wharf Landing?"

"I never pry into where a man gets his money."

"Is he in the kidnapping business?"

"I have no idea what you're talking about."

"Did he lose a Mario Fernández briefcase containing a lot of money?"

"Who's Mario Fernández?"

I'll say one thing for Adriana Vargas, she's a difficult woman to fluster. She didn't so much as blink while I threw questions at her. "How did you get to be the director here?"

"I was friendly with one of the investors."

"Which one?"

"Again, none of your business."

"Why keep it a secret that you live in Wharf Landing?"

"It's hardly a secret; it seems everyone but you know I live here."

The high ground was working for Adriana, so I decided to fire a shot from below. I took out my phone, pulled up the photo Hans had given me and held it up for her to see. I pointed to the man I identified as the jumper. "This is the man who was shot in Wharf Landing on August 22nd. What's his name?"

She tried to keep cool, but I could tell her blood was beginning to boil. "Where did you get that photo?" she asked.

"It doesn't matter. I have it."

Her mouth moved and although no sound came out it wasn't difficult to read her lips, "that son of a bitch."

"So, what's this man's name?" I asked again.

"I don't know him."

"You're in the picture with him."

"It was taken at a gathering. He must have been someone's guest."

"It looks like all these other guys know him."

"What makes you think that?"

I zoomed in on the right hand of one of the men in the photo. "All of these men, including the one you claim to be a guest, are wearing the same ring. It looks like a fraternal order of some sort and it looks like our victim is a member of the fraternity."

"I have no idea what you're talking about."

I closed the screen. "All those men own a unit at

Wharf Landing, don't they?"

The soft features of her face turned hard and if looks could kill, I would have been dead. "You tell me, you seem to know the answers to your questions before you ask them."

"The man standing next to the victim ... is that Emiliano Muñoz?"

"Unlike you, Dr. Rose, the men who own units in this building are powerful men. If you return to Wharf Landing, I suggest you watch your back."

"Is that a threat?"

"You decide, but this meeting is over."

I left and while heading back to my office I called Jim and told him to get Hans out of Wharf Landing—immediately. I no longer questioned if Adriana Vargas fit the profile of a killer.

CHAPTER FORTY-TWO

E instein woke me with a stroke of his sandpaper tongue across my cheek and I rewarded him with a couple of four-letter words and a bowl of Fancy Feast Seafood Pâté. Then I stepped outside to pick up the morning *Chronicle*. I wasn't crazy about how the publisher covered the local news, but I was addicted to The Green Sheet, their sports section. Before I could reach for the paper a taxi pulled up in front of my house and honked. It looked familiar. So did the driver. "Hey Doc, it's Bruno, can I talk to you for a few minutes?"

For a guy who just had a quarter of a million-dollar windfall, he didn't look very happy. "Sure, come on in, I'll buy you a cup a coffee." I filled two mugs and we sat at the kitchen table. "How did you know where I lived?"

"I asked Detective Allen and told him it was important I talk to you. I hope that was all right."

It wasn't hard to detect the anguish in his voice. "No problem, it's fine," I said. "So, what is it you want to talk about?"

To say Bruno looked uncomfortable would be an understatement. "I took out the back seat of my cab to clean all the crap that falls behind it and found these." He reached into his jacket pocket and pulled out a pistol and a brass key on a short metal chain.

"The jumper's?" I asked.

"They were wedged in the corner where he was sitting."

"I thought you said he took the gun with him when he went over the rail."

"I said, 'I thought he took it with him.'"

"Okay, well, you were right to bring these to me."

"Am I in trouble?"

"Of course not, why would you think that?"

"A guy I pick up dies from gunshot wound, I have $250,000 of his money and then all of a sudden a gun shows up in my cab."

"That money never existed," I said. Bruno was staring off into space and didn't hear me. I shook his arm and raised my voice. "Bruno, that money never existed, did it?"

He came back to the moment. "No, Doc, it didn't."

"Remember that ... or we'll be sharing a jail cell together."

"I will. What about the gun?"

"Did you touch it?"

He shook his head and pointed at a cloth handkerchief. "Uh, uh, I picked it up with that."

"Good, I'll turn it over to the police. You go home. Your shift ended an hour ago and your wife is probably worried about you."

"What if the cops question me about the gun?"

"Just tell them truth about it. And just so you know, the money that never existed was probably dirty money."

"What's that mean ... dirty?"

"Means a bad person did something bad to get it."

After Bruno left I picked up the gun with the handkerchief and slipped it into a grocery bag. The thought of carrying a gun on a cable car didn't appeal to me, so after a shave and a shower, I summoned an Uber and tapped in Police Headquarters as the destination.

Jim was out on a case, but Mike Kelly was in. I asked if I could see him. As soon as I walked into his office, I set the shopping bag down on his conference table and he handed me a cup of coffee. "Rick, I just asked Jim about your case this morning. He said the woman who manages Wharf Landing is on your radar."

I took a gulp of the sludge that tasted like it was made of molasses. "Adriana Vargas is certainly cold enough to be a killer, but I think this case stretches beyond her. We have a photo of her with nine guys all wearing the same rings. One of them is the guy who worked me over in Colombia and another is our jumper. It looks almost like a secret fraternal order of some kind."

"So, why would they shoot one of their own?"

"Three quarters of a million dollars? People have been shot for a lot less."

Mike leaned back to digest the information, a task much easier than that of the coffee. He pointed to the shopping bag. "You stop off at the supermarket?"

"It's the jumper's gun. The cab driver brought it to my house this morning."

"Where did he get it?"

"He found it wedged behind his back seat. He's afraid of how it will look to the police."

"As far as I know, he's not a suspect, so tell him to relax. What kind of gun?"

I shrugged. "I wouldn't know the difference between a pea shooter and a 357 Magnum."

"No problem, I'll have our weapons team analyze it."

CHAPTER FORTY-THREE

I asked Siri to find me the 'nearest locksmith' and she came up with the Key West Key Shop located at Twenty-first and Valencia Streets—not exactly downtown, but only a ten-minute Uber ride into the Mission District.

I was expecting the owner of the shop to be from Florida, but it turned out his name is Bill West, a perfect name for a play on words. I handed him the chain with the key dangling from it. "Any idea what kind of lock this fits?" I asked.

Bill took out a handheld, monocular magnifying glass that looked like a jeweler's loop. I guess he was left-eyed, because he closed the right one when he held up the magnifier and then brought the key toward him until he had it in focus. "Schlage," he said.

I wasn't sure if that was a foreign language or just lock talk. "Beg your pardon."

"Schlage ... they make the best locks in world." He handed me his loop. "Take a peek."

I focused on the key but had to squint to read the lettering. "SC1, what does that mean?"

"SC is the industry abbreviation for Schlage and the number one is their code for a residential lock."

"So, it's a house key."

"House, condo, apartment … anything residential."

I wanted to pay Bill West for his time, but he wouldn't let me, so instead I handed him one of my cards. "If you ever need a dead body identified, give me a call."

On the ten-minute ride back to my office I tried to piece together what I knew. The jumper was from Colombia, that's where he got the briefcase. Emiliano Muñoz is from Colombia, that's where he had me kidnapped. Adriana Vargas may or may not be from Colombia, but if she's not, she's tied to it somehow. The realtor told me that at Wharf Landing Emiliano Muñoz owns units 605, 604 and 603. Adriana lives in 605 and Emiliano in 604.

Unit 603 was put up for sale two weeks after the jumper was killed. Is it possible he lived there? If the key he left behind fits that front door, it means the jumper, Emiliano and Adriana were cozy neighbors—that is, until the jumper was murdered.

The first thing I did when I got back to my office was to call Jim. He must have recognized my ID and picked up before it rang. "Rick?"

"Yeah, did you get my message?"

"About Hans?"

"Yeah, did you get him out of Wharf Landing?"

"I tried, but nobody's seen him."

"You mean he skipped again?"

"Or worse."

"Oh, shit."

"Hopefully he's back in Santa Fe, hanging out with his girlfriend."

"I hope so. Hey, I need your help with something else."

"What's that?"

"We need to get into Wharf Landing tonight ... without being seen."

~ * ~

Normally a doorman was out front 24/7, but if for some reason he wasn't there, the tenants would need a way to get in. If Wharf Landing was like other condominiums, the key to a tenant's unit would also fit the building's front door.

We decided the best time to sneak in would be between two and three a.m. Jim picked me up at two-thirty. He made a slow pass and I spotted Sam Woodruff, the uncooperative doorman, standing inside one of the glass doors. As soon as we were out of sight, Jim pulled to a stop and we got out. He headed to the front door and I snuck along the dark side of the building.

As we planned, I watched Jim show his credentials to Woodruff and after what appeared to be an argument, the doorman followed Jim to his police car. As soon as they were out of sight I hurried to the front door. I wiggled the key into the lock, turned it, and heard a click. I scrambled inside the rotunda.

The chance that someone might be using the elevator at this hour was slim; the chance they would be using the stairs was close to zero. I went straight for the door leading to the stairwell and by the time I reached the 6th floor I was sucking for air. The hallway was dimly lit but illuminated enough to recognize the unit numbers. I headed to the door of 603 and inserted the key. It slid in smoothly. I stepped inside.

It was like going into a mausoleum—cold and musty. I lit up the flashlight on my phone and began scanning the living room. It was empty and so were the adjoining den and kitchen. I aimed the beam at the master bedroom and stepped in. It was empty too.

There was nothing more to see, so I returned to the living room and headed for the door. A voice echoed from a dark corner. "Looking for something?"

I don't know how I kept from peeing in my pants, but somehow, I did. "Who … who are you?" I asked.

A man stepped from the shadows into my beam of light. "Isn't it a little late to be house hunting, Dr. Rose?" It was Mr. Big from Colombia and he was holding a pistol— one that looked exactly like the one Bruno found behind his seat.

I managed to collect my wits. "Mr. Emiliano Muñoz, I presume."

"I asked you politely to drop your investigation, do you remember?"

"I remember, but I couldn't do it. It's my job. Are you going to shoot me for doing my job?"

"Possibly. Did you find the whereabouts of a second briefcase?"

"I told you, I don't know anything about a second briefcase."

"I think you are lying to me, just as you were in Cartagena. Was my message not strong enough?"

"Yes, it was. It was very strong. But I can't tell you what I don't know."

He wasn't fazed and aimed the gun at my groin. "I'll count to ten. Where is the second briefcase?"

I closed my eyes listening to … six, five, four … and waiting for the sound of a gunshot and the rush of pain that would follow. Instead, I heard the front door open. "That's enough tough guy shit," Jim said.

I opened my eyes. Emiliano Muñoz continued to aim the pistol at my crotch while he talked to Jim. "Sir, this property belongs to me and this man has entered it without my permission. I have every right to shoot him."

Jim held up his badge. "In Colombia maybe, but not here." He looked my way. "Come on, Rick, we're leaving."

CHAPTER FORTY-FOUR

By the time we were back in Jim's police car it was after 4:00 a.m. and my mood matched the weather—dark and dreary. Jim turned on the wipers to remove the condensation of fog from his windshield, while I closed my eyes and tried to erase the evening. "Sorry," I said.

"For what?"

"For you having to save my butt."

"What's your problem?"

"I feel like a kid whose daddy had to drive him home from a date."

"Come on, man, they pay me to save butts. Besides, this was a productive night."

"How d'ya figure? We're not any closer to knowing who the jumper was or who killed him."

"I disagree."

"Meaning?"

"The jumper's key fit the lock to unit 603, which means your hunch was correct … he lived there. That means Emiliano Muñoz knows the ID of the jumper and considering the proximity of their apartments, so does Adriana Vargas. You think you can figure out their connection?"

All of a sudden I was wide awake. "I think I may have a way."

"Good, do it. Before you went into your self-pity funk, I was going to tell you what I discovered tonight."

"From the doorman?"

"Yup, I locked him in the back seat of the car and told him I was bringing him down to the station for questioning. He caved."

"He admitted seeing the jumper?"

"He saw him all right. He recognized him as one of the tenants, but he didn't know his name. The guy looked awful and was having trouble walking. The doorman asked if he was okay, but he passed him without a reply and headed toward a cab parked at the curb."

"Why didn't he tell us this before?"

"Adriana Vargas told him to dummy up or he'd lose his job."

"That's good stuff, Jim."

"That is good stuff, but I have some better stuff."

My heart began pumping like it does after a second double espresso. "Well, let's hear it."

"The doorman took a bathroom break about ten minutes before the jumper hobbled out and when he returned to his post, he saw the back of a man who must have come out of the building while he was gone. The guy was in a hurry and carrying a leather briefcase. It looked just like the one the jumper was carrying when he came out."

"A second briefcase? Did he recognize the guy?"

"He couldn't see his face and thought he might be a tenant. He just couldn't make out which one."

Jim turned on Beach Street, two blocks west of Hyde. The cable car had stopped running at 11:00 p.m. and it was now almost 4:00 a.m. so parking wasn't a problem. He pulled up to the curb in front of my house. "See you tomorrow," he said.

I opened the car door and glanced up at my front window. "It is tomorrow ... and it looks like my cat is hungry."

CHAPTER FORTY-FIVE

I slept in and when I rolled into the office around noon, Stella was on her way out. She looked at her watch. "I guess Frankie returned your call."

I winced. "No, I haven't heard from her, I was up late working on the jumper case."

"Wanna go to lunch?"

"I'd like to, but I have to talk to Helmut. Raincheck?"

"Sure, see ya later."

As she always does, Stella sorted my mail into a neat pile. Most of it was junk and I threw everything out except for a Westin Hotel promo offer—5 days, 4 nights in Cabo San Lucas for $199. All I'd have to do is sit through an hour sales pitch to buy a timeshare. Maybe after this case is over, I'll take Frankie down there, I thought. That is, if she ever calls me.

I was about to head down to the morgue when my phone buzzed. I recognized the ID. "Mike, what's up?"

"I have some interesting news. I just got a call from my weapons team. The pistol your cab driver found was made in Colombia, a 9mm INDUMIL Córdova."

"That's the same type that killed the jumper."

"How do you know?"

"Helmut's ballistics guy identified the bullet as coming from a 9mm INDUMIL Córdova."

"You don't think he shot himself."

"I doubt it."

~ * ~

I didn't bother to call the morgue to see if Helmut was there; he was always there. When I stepped in, I was greeted by one of the Brandenburg concertos blaring though the speakers. Helmut didn't hear the door open and when I tapped him on the shoulder, while he was in the middle of his autopsy, he almost jumped out of his surgical scrubs. "Rick, don't do that, I could have made the wrong incision."

"Don't worry, I doubt your patient will sue. Hey, I need a favor."

He stripped off his mask and gloves and pulled a sheet over the cadaver. "Sure, what's up?"

"Do you still have that $10,000 microscope?"

"You mean the Zeiss Discovery.V8 Stereo?"

"Yeah, that's it."

"It's worth more than ten grand now, but, yes, I still have it."

"Great, would you put the ring you took off the jumper's finger under the scope?"

He located the ring and we stepped over to a table housing five microscopes. The Zeiss Discovery.V8 Stereo was the flagship. It took a good ten minutes for Helmut to program the settings and get the stage ready, then he locked the ring into position and brought it into focus. "What are we looking for?" he asked.

"Whatever we see."

He stepped away and motioned me toward the eyepiece. "It's all yours."

I adjusted the focus. There were several small gemstones, a few diamonds, a ruby and a couple emeralds, but under them, engraved in tiny letters, was written, *populum defendere MMXXII.* "You know any Latin?" I asked.

"Yes, I got straight A's in Latin. Why?"

I pointed to the eyepiece. "What does this phrase mean?"

Helmut tweaked the scope. "Huh, *populum defendere.* A loose interpretation would be, 'protecting the people.' And *MMXXII* are the Roman numerals for the year 2022."

"So, 'protecting the people 2022.'"

"Pretty close."

My cell was one step above a flip top but Helmut, a computer nerd, had a new iPhone 15 Pro Max. Can I borrow your phone?" I asked. He handed it to me and I said, "Siri, what organization uses *populum defendere* as a motto?" In five seconds she spit out, "Colombia National Police."

A couple thoughts were floating around my brain, but I couldn't quite put them together. Then they collided. "Helmut, you said the gun that killed the jumper was used by the Colombian military." I handed back his phone. "See who else uses that gun."

He tapped a few keys and held the display up for me to see. "*The INDUMIL Córdova is a weapon recently developed for use by the Colombia National Police.*"

~ * ~

I returned to my office and bumped into Stella coming back from lunch. It was my turn to look at my watch. "Two hours, a nooner?"

"Oh, Rick, don't be silly, it was just a long lunch."

I cocked my head and squinted. "At MoMo's, by any chance?"

"We're back together."

"You and Maverick."

"Uh, huh."

"I thought that was over."

"It was until you took me back there last week. He's so cute."

I never could understand relationships. What attracts one person to another is like an unknown in an algebra problem. You don't get the answer before figuring out the entire equation. "Well, I'm happy for you," I said. I felt my phone vibrate in my pocket and took it out to check the ID. "Stella, I have to take this, we'll talk later."

I stepped into my office and felt my stomach tighten as I tapped the green circle on the screen. "Frankie?"

"*Allô*, Rick."

"I've been hoping you would call."

"I apologize. My father's heart condition has taken a turn for the worse and I've had to be in constant touch with my mother."

"Oh, I'm sorry, how bad is it?"

Her voice wavered. "Very bad ... Rick, I'm going back to France."

"And you should. Any idea how long you'll be gone?" There was a silent pause. "Frankie, are you still there?"

"Yes, I'm here ... Rick, I'm not sure I'll be back."

My body felt like a balloon that had lost all its helium. "But, why?"

"I don't know if I told you, but I'm an only child. My mother will be alone if my father ..." I could hear her crying.

"When do you leave?"

"Tonight."

"Can I take you to the airport?"

"I don't think that would be a good idea."

I didn't want to hear the answer to my next question, but I asked it anyway. "Will you call me?"

There was another silent pause. This time I didn't interrupt and waited for her answer. "I care for you, Rick, and I know you care for me, but I have a lot of thinking to do." I could sense she was framing her next line carefully. "Rick, if I decide not to return, a call will only hurt us both." *Au revoir mon amour*." She hung up. I was numb. I went home early.

CHAPTER FORTY-SIX

I have no idea how the internet works, but it does. Google is its most popular search engine and I have no idea how it works either, but it does. I googled 'Colombia National Police' and the search engine did what it always does—provide more information than is needed.

I wasn't interested in when the National Police Force was formed, how it functioned during the civil wars, or where in the country their academies are located. I was only interested in why *populum defendere MMXXII* was inscribed on the jumper's ring and probably on those of the other men in the Wharf Landing photo.

I already knew that 'protecting the people' is the motto of Colombia's National Police Force, but I didn't know the significance of 2022. I went to their website and typed '2022' into their search box. What filled the screen took my breath away. It was an excerpt from an article published by, *El Tiempo,* Colombia's largest newspaper.

"… 26 April 2022, the leader of the Colombia National Police, and eight members of his staff were released from La Picota prison after serving 15 months for accepting bribes from several drug cartels. Attorney General, Juan Moreno Rojas, consented to the reduced sentences after all nine men agreed to resign from the force and plead guilty…"

Nine full face pictures followed the article. The name under the first picture was that of the leader—*General Emiliano Muñoz Garcia*. And under the next, who unmistakenly was the jumper—*Javier Vargas Ferreira*.

I remembered the tutorial the manager of the leather store in Bogotá had given me. In Colombia after your first name comes your father's surname followed by your mother's surname.

If these two men had dropped their mother's surnames after coming to America, they would be known here as Emiliano Muñoz and Javier Vargas. And if Adriana Vargas had done the same, that would make her the jumper's sister. What I couldn't figure out was the relationship of Emiliano Muñoz to Adriana Vargas and how they might be involved in the death of her brother, Javier. I needed to talk to Alex.

Her secretary waved me on through, where Alex was working at her desk. "Well, look what the cat dragged in," she said.

"Einstein would take offense to that. ... house cats never drag anything in. Hey, sorry I've been incommunicado. I've been totally consumed by this case."

"Apology accepted. How's it going?"

"Well, you being the medical examiner, I'm officially informing you that I've identified the guy who jumped off the Golden Gate Bridge."

A big smile lit up her face. "That's fantastic, who was he?"

"His name is Javier Vargas. He was from Colombia, but he was living in Wharf Landing along with several other associates."

"Is there someone in Colombia who can accept his remains?"

"There's someone right here in the U.S. His sister, Adriana Vargas, is the director of Wharf Landing."

Alex stepped around her desk and gave me a hug. "Rick, I'm proud of you, I knew you would do it. Ready for a new case?"

I wasn't sure how to answer. Technically, my involvement in this case was over, but there were so many questions left unanswered. "Alex, don't you want to know why the jumper was in the U.S., why he had a case full of money and who put a bullet in him?"

"Of course, but it's not our job to find that out, it's the police department's."

"I understand that, but no one, not even Jim Allen nor Mike Kelly, knows this case like I do. Let me stay on it."

Alex didn't answer right away. I'm sure she was weighing not only the ethical implications but also the budgetary ones. "I'm afraid not, Rick. After you notify the sister, your job is done."

"I've got a vacation coming. I'm going start it tomorrow."

"Rick …"

"Alex … please."

She threw up her hands. "Okay, enjoy your vacation."

CHAPTER FORTY-SEVEN

I was lucky to find both Mike Kelly and Jim Allen in police headquarters at the same time. We huddled together around Mike's conference table. "You must have found something good to capture both of us at once," Mike said.

I opened my laptop, brought up the article from the Colombian newspaper and edged the screen to where they both could see it. "Look familiar?" I asked.

"Holy, shit ... a general," Jim said. "So, that's why Muñoz acts like such a big shot."

"Look at the next photo."

"Is that ...."

"The jumper," I said. "His name is Javier Vargas."

"Vargas?"

"Adriana's brother."

"Who are these other seven guys?"

"The same men Adriana is posing with in the picture on her end table. I think if we check the owners at Wharf Landing again, we'll find that all these men live on the fifth and sixth floors."

"And, one of them must own a 9mm INDUMIL Córdova," Mike said.

That brought up the memory of my night at Wharf

Landing, when Emiliano Muñoz threatened to shoot me with one. "Mike, after I inform Adriana that we've identified her brother as the jumper, the medical examiner's job is over, but if it's all right with you, I'd like to stay on until your case is closed."

Mike gave me a questioning look. "I assume you've discussed this with Alex, what did she have to say about it?"

"She said, 'enjoy your vacation,' so I guess now I qualify as one of your confidential informants."

"You sure you want to do this?"

"Positive."

"Okay then." He turned to Jim. "Tell Rick what you found out about our other CI."

Jim had the look of a guy whose game winning kick just bounced off the upright. "Turns out this guy is a much better grifter than we gave him credit for. He conned us."

"Conned us? How?"

"Hans hasn't been back to Wharf Landing since the night of the shooting."

"That's impossible, you ordered him to go back and he brought us the photo he took of that picture on Adriana's end table."

"That wasn't a photo of a picture. That photo was an original."

"Hans took it himself?"

"That's right. I gave my copy to our lab for analysis and they confirmed it. They even found a deleted time stamp, August 22, 2023 - 2:46 a.m."

In my four years with the medical examiner's office, I've had to process a lot of unbelievable information, but what I had just heard was almost impossible to work through. It was inconceivable that a small-time con man, like Hans Van den Brink, could work his way into the circle of high-powered Colombian gangsters and on the night of the shooting at Wharf Landing snap a posed photo of all nine of them. Even more mind blowing, he was able to con not only me, but a detective from the San Francisco police department into believing he was co-operating with him. "Have you located him yet?" I asked.

"Yeah, he was on a plane to Venezuela two hours after he gave us the photo. A source there says he's living it up in a 5-star hotel called the Cayena Caracas."

"Caracas? Why Venezuela?"

"Maybe because they don't have extradition with the U.S."

"What's he running from? Not a $10,000 scam on a coffee truck owner."

Mike interrupted. "Hey, guys, remember our job. It's to find the person who put the bullet from an INDUMIL Córdova into the jumper?"

Jim, never shy on voicing his opinion said, "Colombian victim, Colombian money, Colombian gun. I'm going with a Colombian shooter. A guy named Emiliano Muñoz."

I was still conflicted. "What was Hans doing there on August 22nd?" I said.

Jim voiced another opinion. "Doing what a vulture always does, waiting to come in after the kill to pick up the stray meat."

I knew the jumper's briefcase originally contained a million dollars, so it wasn't such an audacious assumption to believe that another case may have also. "The stray meat being the second briefcase," I said.

Jim smiled. "If the shoe fits."

Mike looked at me. "Is that what you think, Rick?"

I wasn't as quick to make a decision as Jim was. "It's no secret Emiliano Muñoz owns an INDUMIL Córdova, but I'm guessing so do a lot of other guys on the fifth and sixth floors. As far as stealing a briefcase full of money from the Colombians, I don't think Hans would have the balls for it."

"When are you paying a visit to Adriana Vargas to let her know about her brother?" Mike asked me.

"First thing tomorrow. Now that we know he was the jumper, maybe she'll be more inclined to tell me what happened to him at Wharf Landing on the night of August 22nd."

"I'll go with you," Jim said.

"No, she dislikes you even more than she does me. I can handle it."

He smirked. "Hey, last time you were there alone, Emiliano Muñoz almost shot you."

"But he didn't."

"Because I stopped him."

"Jim, I think I can get through to Adriana. Let me go alone. I'll be fine."

CHAPTER FORTY-EIGHT

S am Woodruff, the usual late-night doorman, met me at the entry to Wharf Landing. "Working early today?" I asked.

"Yes, sir, I switched shifts."

I showed my credentials. "Rick Rose, I have an appointment with Ms. Vargas."

"Yes, sir, I remember you." He pushed open the door, but before I could pass through, he said, "Please ... don't tell her I talked to the detective."

I nodded. "No worries."

I knew how tough Adriana could be, so I put on my emotional armor when her secretary showed me in. As usual, Adriana didn't smile but she didn't shoot daggers at me either. Instead of seating me across a desk from her, she pointed to a couple of chairs next to a small table where a carafe and a half a dozen cups were sitting. "Coffee?" she asked.

"Sure, two sugars."

She stirred the cups and passed one to me. "Dr. Rose, you're more courageous than I thought. After our last meeting, I didn't think I'd see you here without a police escort.

"I didn't take your threat seriously. Should I have?"

She thought about the question before answering. "I guess that depends on your reason for coming back."

"I've identified the jumper. Is that a good enough reason?"

"Then, you know."

"I know he was your brother, if that's what you mean."

She remained stoic. "So, what's next?"

"Are you going to claim the body?"

"I'm not sure."

"Why, because of the briefcase?"

"What briefcase?"

"I think you know what briefcase."

"I'm sorry, I don't."

I set my cup on the table and stood up. "Look, Adriana, I don't really give a damn if you want your brother back; we can bury him without you. But I think somehow you and Emiliano are in a tight spot and if you stop lying to me, I might be able to help you." I dropped a fresh business card on the table. "Call me if you change your mind." I started for the door.

"Wait," she said. I turned but didn't speak. "Sit back down ... please."

I did as she asked and we sat in silence for about a minute or two before she spoke again. "We do want my brother back, but how can we claim him? We'd have to answer for why he was carrying a million dollars of undeclared cash inside a briefcase."

"And, why was he?" I asked.

"He wanted to give it away."

"I don't get it."

"Did you know he was dying?"

"Of course, I found the tumor during my examination."

Adriana stood, went to the window, and stared out at the fog that was forming across the bay. Without looking at me, she said, "Do you know where that money came from?"

"I have a pretty good idea. It came from bribes while he was on the Colombia National Police force."

She didn't confirm or deny it, instead she turned and said, "If you had met Javier, you would have known, despite his transgressions, he was a very religious person. After he learned he was dying, he was convinced he'd be eternally separated from his God."

"You mean he believed he was going to hell."

The hint of a smile crept into her face. "He thought by giving the money to people who needed it, he might earn some absolution."

We heard a knock at Adriana's door, but before she could respond, Emiliano Muñoz stepped in with a face full of fury. "Adriana, what are telling this man?" he said.

"It's all right, Emil, he knows it was Javier who jumped off the bridge."

"It's not all right. He works for the government."

"Mr. Muñoz," I said. "I don't work for the U.S. government, I work for the local medical examiner. My job was to identify the man who jumped off the Golden Gate Bridge. I've done that. My job is finished."

"I checked, you do work for the government—the government of San Francisco."

"It's not the United States government. We don't care that you and Javier brought $2,000,000 into the country without declaring it, and the police department really doesn't care either. They just want to find the person who shot and killed Javier."

The blood that was boiling in Emiliano's face cooled and he sighed a sigh of resignation. He spotted the carafe on the table, poured himself a cup and took a large gulp. "Ah, Colombian, finest coffee in the world, don't you agree?" I knew the question was rhetorical. "Did Adriana tell you that Javier had this crazy idea to give his money away?" he asked.

"She did, but she didn't tell me who shot him." I paused before the next question. "Was it you … to keep him from doing it?"

To my surprise, he broke out laughing. "You're not as good a detective as I gave you credit for, Dr. Rose. If you were, you'd know Adriana is my niece and Javier my nephew. I raised them after my brother and his wife died. When that nasty business in Colombia was over, I bought all of us apartments here in Wharf Landing."

He was right, I wasn't a good detective—never claimed to be. I'd come this far and still didn't know who shot the jumper. "What happened here on the night of August 22nd?" I asked.

Emiliano ran his fingers through his hair and slowly shook his head as if that might erase a painful memory. "My nephew was a private person and didn't tell us about the tumor until it was too late. We all knew he was dying. August 22nd was his going away party."

I wasn't sure what he meant by 'going away.' "So, he decided to jump after the party?"

"Not exactly," Emiliano replied. "We'd said our good-byes weeks ago and left it up to him to decide when he would slip away and do it. But after the party the decision was made for him."

I didn't think Adriana was capable of it, but she began

to cry. Emiliano patted her shoulder and turned to me. "I'll tell you what happened that night, if you promise we can claim Javier's body without blowback from the police department."

"You know the police have Javier's money and there's nothing I can do to get it back to you. It's going to charity."

"Yes, I suspected as much, but it was his to do with as he wished. He'd no doubt be pleased."

I'd already made one promise that had gotten me into deep trouble, so one more couldn't make it much worse. "Okay, I'll make sure Javier comes back to you without any strings," I said.

He took out a pack of cigarettes, then decided against it and laid them on the table. "I invited most of the Wharf Landing owners to the party and the rum and tequila were flowing. Javier had too much of both and his tongue began to flow more than the alcohol. I tried to stop him, but he let out our secret that two briefcases full of money, which we'd taken from Colombia, were in his apartment."

"That bastard shot him," Adriana yelled.

Emiliano patted her shoulder again. "He must have slipped into my bedroom, taken one of my INDUMIL Córdovas and after the party was over, gone to Javier's apartment. We heard a gunshot and when we realized it came from #603, we ran to it. There was blood on the floor, Javier was gone and so were the two briefcases."

"But Javier only had one of them when he got into the cab," I said.

"Hans Van den Brink has the other."

It was like a gut punch. A two-bit con man outsmarted not only the cops, but also the robbers. "How? How do you know it was him?"

Adriana, who now had her emotions back in check,

said, "We didn't until you showed me that photo a couple of days ago."

"I don't understand."

"We were pretty drunk by the end of the party and we thought one of Emiliano's co-conspirators was the shooter. After all, they were the last to leave the party, they had just heard about the money, and they knew where Javier's apartment was located. When you held up the photo of me standing next to all of them, I remembered it was taken just minutes before they left, so there was one other person still at the party."

"The photographer," I said.

Emiliano nodded. "Now he has disappeared and so has the second briefcase."

If emotions of relief and anger could erupt at the same time, they did so in me. I could leave this conversation as is and walk away without fear of retribution from Emiliano. But making my blood curdle was knowing Hans would get away with murder along with a briefcase containing $1,000,000. "Does Colombia share a border with Venezuela?" I asked.

Emiliano looked perplexed. "Yes."

"So, do your associates in Colombia have influence inside that country?"

"Yes, why?"

"Have them check out the Cayena Caracas hotel. They'll find everything you're looking for."

CHAPTER FORTY-NINE

For the first time in over a month, I had a good night's sleep without having to get up and go into the office the next morning. After all, I was on vacation. I toasted a bagel and took it into the living room along with a cup of Colombian coffee. I was beginning to like the stuff.

Einstein jumped on my lap and began kneading his claws against my pajamas, but I brushed him aside and flipped on the TV. A commentator on the Channel 4 *Morning News* was finishing a story and I was able to catch his last words "... found dead in a hotel in Caracas, Venezuela ..." I felt no guilt, no remorse.

It's often been said that a bachelor's life is a carefree and independent one. What hasn't been said is that it's usually a lonely one too. It was especially true today, when I had a victory lap to take and no one to take it with.

I called Alex, told her the news and asked her to join me for lunch, but she already had one scheduled with her boss, the mayor. Stella was always up for a free lunch, but Maverick had beat me to it and was taking her to Ghirardelli Square for seafood chowder.

I closed my eyes and fell back asleep but woke with a start when my phone began vibrating its way to the end of the coffee table. I grabbed it, hit the green circle on the screen, and put it to my ear. "Hello?"

"*Allô,* Rick."

ACKNOWLEDGEMENTS

I've thanked them many times before, but I will do it again. They're the people who, over the years, have become regular players on 'my team.' They read my working manuscripts and see what I don't see while writing them: Brad Liebman,who hates to criticize, but for my sake does. Scott Paulo, a mathematician in his previous life and luckily for me, a nitpicker in this one. Barrie Scheid, my daughter who has the guts to tell me when something I write sounds bad. And finally, my wife, Bev, who continues to be my biggest fan and staunchest critic.

I also wish to thank fellow authors, Lynn Solte, Ann Marie Jameson and Jack Lawson, who lent their time to read the manuscript and write short reviews, which are included in this published product.

As always, my thanks to my editor, Jeanne Smith and cover artist, Trisha FitzGerald-Jung. One last shout-out to Linda Voth, CEO of Wings ePress, who retired this year. Thanks, Linda, for jump starting my works into publication.

MEET MIKE PAULL

In the year 2000, Mike Paull retired from the practice of dentistry in the San Francisco Bay Area and began honing his skills as a writer. Between 2010 and 2015 he published *Tales from the Sky Kitchen Café,* a book of aviation-based short stories and a three-volume mystery series: *Flight of Betrayal, Flight of Deception* and *Flight of no Return.*

Beginning in 2021, Mike partnered with Wings ePress, an independent U.S. publisher. Over the next three years they released his spy thriller series: *Missing, She's Missing* and *Missing in the Maldives.*

In 2024, Mike introduced *The Mouth Mechanic,* a forensic crime novel. He called on his dental background to create the character of Rick Rose, a young dentist who after losing his license, ends up in the San Francisco morgue solving the mystery of a man whose body rolled out of a restaurant dumpster.

The Head Case is Book II in the Rick Rose series. It follows the protagonist through a wild adventure as he scrambles to identify and find the story behind a disembodied head that has washed ashore on a San Francisco beach.

You have just read *The Jumper*, Book III in the series, where Rick solves the mystery of an unidentified man who, after being shot in the chest, jumps off the Golden Gate Bridge.

Mike and his wife Bev now live near family in Chico CA, two hundred miles north of San Francisco.

OTHER WORKS BY MIKE PAULL

Missing - A bullet to the back detours a government agent's search for a hidden stash of gold.

She's Missing - When an intelligence agent's old partner goes missing, he puts his life on the line to find her.

Missing in the Maldives - While looking for the man who shot them six months ago, two U.S. intelligence officers search islands in the Indian Ocean only to get entangled in a web from which escape is difficult.

The Mouth Mechanic - After losing his license to alcohol, a young dentist finds himself in the morgue investigating the identity of a murder victim.

The Head Case - A disembodied head washes up on a San Francisco beach, and leads Rick Rose, a forensic dentist, on a dangerous journey to identify it.

www.ingramcontent.com/pod-product-compliance
Lightning Source LLC
Chambersburg PA
CBHW060542260626
47161CB00003B/1020